TRAIN TO MIDNIGHT

A Dream-Quest Adventure

Janie Lynn Panagopoulos

River Road Publications, Inc.

Spring Lake, Michigan

ISBN: 0-938682-53-9

Printed in the United States of America

Dedication

Several important people have made a difference in my life and in the way I look at education and learning. I would like dedicate this book to them and to thank them for their encouragement. They have inspired me to make learning a life-long pursuit.

My mother, Betty Blount, has given me a true sense of myself and of the importance of learning. She has always supported my interests and even now encourages all my efforts. Thank you.

Also, my thanks to several educators from my elementary school, Washington Elementary School in Owosso, Michigan. Over thirty years ago they made learning an enjoyable journey. They were good role models; some were tough, some nurturing, some challenged my mind to the point of frustration, but in their own way each taught me to "love" learning. Thank you, Irma Cottonham, Catherine Reif, Lucille Richardson, Carol Johnson, Pauline Bach and Richard Forsyth.

And, just a reminder to all the wonderful teachers in the world: every day, in some way, you are touching and changing the lives of young people. Keep up the good work!

Contents

Chapter 1   The Underground Railroad   1

Chapter 2   The Fire-eater   15

Chapter 3   A Friend in Need   25

Chapter 4   The Meeting   37

Chapter 5   Pattyrollers ... .,,...............   52

Chapter 6   Night Travelers   67

Chapter 7   Unwelcome Guests   78

Chapter 8   An Underground Rest   91

Chapter 9   Albie 100

Chapter 10 Train to Midnight 116

Chapter 11 Detroit 135

Chapter 12 Escape 149

Chapter 13 Homeward Bound 161

Glossary   ....,167

Underground Railroad Sites 175

A Note From
Janie Lynn Panagopoulos

I first became interested in studying the Underground Railroad while doing research in Albany, New York for *Erie Trail West*. Some of the material that I read contained shocking and heart-breaking stories of people traveling the Underground Railroad in New York.

Upon further research, I realized that this very important part of our American heritage had, in some ways, been forgotten. I realized that each state had its own story to tell. This sent me on a quest which ultimately led to this book.

The story of slavery and the Underground Railroad and it consequences to our nation are far reaching. The bravery of those who sought freedom for themselves, their families, and their future was incredible.

What I like most about the Underground Railroad is that it is a story about courage and strength. It is about people standing up for their rights and the rights of others while turning their backs on popular opinions. These people were not afraid to do the right thing. That, in itself, makes me proud to be an American.

I like to think that if I had lived at that time, I

would have been one of those that helped, perhaps as an Abolitionist and a friend of freedom. I also believe that those often humble helpers of the Underground Railroad were some of our most important American heroes, and I applaud them.

A special note of thanks to:

Miss Malaika Hally, daughter of Franklin and Onani Hally of Yellow Springs, Ohio for use of her first name for one of my main characters.

Miss Olivia Chambers, daughter of Mark and Jody Chambers of Mackinac Island, Michigan for the use of her first name for the wife of the Quaker, Enos.

Also a special thanks to the fine staff at the Milton House Museum, Milton, Wisconsin for their help, interest, and dedication to the history of the Underground Railroad.

"Lunda lukongolo lwa lunga."

(Keep your circle complete.)

*A northern Angolan / Western Zairean proverb
for safety and well being.*

Chapter 1

The Underground Railroad

"No, it isn't!"

"Uh huh, it is too!"

"Sammy, you don't even know what you're talking about! Give me back my ball of braided string." Malaika (Ma-la-ka) reached out, sticking her hand in Sammy's face. "Mr. Daniels taught us all about the **Underground Railroad** today, and it doesn't run underground!"

"Yes, it does, that's why it's called the Underground Railroad: just like a subway, it runs underground. Here's your dumb old ball of string. It isn't good for anything anyway, except playing with the cat."

"It's not a dumb ball of string, it's part of a slave story. And I better not catch you giving it to the cat."

Malaika grabbed the multi-colored ball of braided string from her brother's hand. "Close your locker and get your backpack," she snapped. "You can ask Mr. Daniels yourself. He'll tell you that the

Underground Railroad don't run under no ground."

"We can't go see Mr. Daniels," protested Sammy. "We have to catch our bus."

"That's why you got to hurry up. Now, shut that locker door, so we can go!"

Sammy grabbed his backpack and slung it up onto his shoulder. With his foot he booted the locker shut.

"What do you have that stupid stuffed cat sticking out of your backpack for?" asked Malaika. The face of an orange and black striped cat peered out at her, almost whacking her in the nose.

Sammy shrugged. "What's wrong, don't you like my cat? You just wish you had one. That's all."

"You're crazy! Now come on, before Mr. Daniels leaves."

"We're gonna miss the bus," argued Sammy. "Mama will be real mad if we miss our bus."

"Come on!" Malaika grabbed her brother's backpack, yanking him sideways down the hall at top speed. The stuffed cat bobbed back and forth as they ran.

"Slow down! Stop yanking me around!"

"You don't want to miss that bus, now do you?" she asked.

"I'm gonna tell Mama on you."

"You be quiet!" Malaika hissed as she dragged her brother down the hallway.

Just 'cause he's a boy, he thinks he's so smart, Malaika thought to herself. Which is crazy, since I'm in fifth grade and he's only in fourth. I'll show him who's smart. Mr. Daniels will set him straight.

At the lockers near Mr. Daniels' room, a group of Sammy's friends stood talking. When they spied Sammy being dragged down the hall by Malaika, they laughed and called to him.

"Sammy, you sure got a real mean sister."

"Malaika, you're a big bully! Why don't you leave Sammy alone? He ain't done nothing to you!"

"Sammy, you gonna let a girl pull you around like that?"

"I know, she's mean," Sammy called back. "She's always mean to me. See, Malaika, everyone thinks you're a big bully-girl."

"Be quiet, you. Just be quiet!" Malaika jerked hard on Sammy's backpack as she pulled him through Mr. Daniels' doorway and into the classroom.

Outside in the hall the boys raised their voices, pretending to be Malaika, as they laughed and mocked her. "Sammy, no, you just be quiet!"

"You hear me Sammy? Now, you just better

hush!" they teased.

Sammy pulled away from Malaika in anger. "You just wait until we get home. I'm gonna tell Mama, and she's gonna ground you for life!" Sammy snarled a smile at the thought.

Malaika lurched forward at her brother, her eyes all squinty and her mouth puckered up. "Now ask him!" she shouted as she pushed her brother in front of Mr. Daniels.

"Hey, hey, Malaika, that isn't a nice way to treat your brother. You shouldn't be pulling him around like that." Mr. Daniels put down the chalk eraser and dusted the chalk from his hands. His big, bristly mustache wiggled when he spoke.

"See!" Sammy turned to his sister, tilting his chin up and grinning smugly.

Malaika lifted her hand towards her brother. In her fist was her ball of multi-colored string.

"Malaika, that's not nice. I see you still have your string. Did you tell Sammy about the story we read today in class?"

"No, not yet. I tried, but Sammy thinks he knows everything about the Underground Railroad. He said it was a subway, under the ground. Tell him what you said, Sammy."

Sammy stood silent and looked down at his feet.

"Sammy, tell him what you said." Malaika nudged her brother sharply with her elbow.

Sammy still stood silent. Malaika's brown eyes glinted with anger. "I can't believe you. You always got something to say. Now, you can't talk? What's wrong with you?

"Mr. Daniels, would you please tell Sammy that the Underground Railroad didn't run under the ground like a subway?"

"She's right, Sammy." Mr. Daniels ran his hand across his face and mustache, leaving a streak of chalk dust behind. Malaika grinned and looked over at Sammy who was still studying his feet.

"The Underground Railroad was the **trackless train,** a secret route for escaped slaves before the Civil War — a secret route to the freedom of the north. There were no subways back then, so runaways traveled any way they could, walking, riding horses, hiding in wagons, and by train and boat. But there were no subways."

"See! I told you so." Malaika smiled with the satisfaction of proving her brother wrong.

Sammy looked up, trying to ignore his sister. Surprised to see the chalk dust on Mr. Daniels' face and mustache, Sammy bit his lower lip so as not to giggle.

"Don't you two have a bus to catch? It looks like it's going to rain and you don't want to walk home in the rain, do you? I sure wouldn't want to, anyway."

Malaika gazed out the classroom windows. Mr. Daniels was right. It did look like it was going to rain.

"Sammy, you have Malaika tell you the story about the string and why it was our special project to make in class today. It really is an interesting story."

Sammy looked up silently at Mr. Daniels and smiled. He is a nice teacher, even with chalk dust on his face, thought Sammy.

Just then, from outside the classroom window, a low rumble of thunder rolled over the school. Gray clouds were passing quickly overhead, casting shadows through the window and making the classroom dark. Mr. Daniels flipped on the light-switch. The fluorescent bulbs snapped and blinked a couple times, and then flashed on, lighting the room.

"And Malaika, be nice to your brother. He's your family. Remember what we learned in the story today? Taking care of one another is one of the most important things in the world."

"Come on, let's go," said Malaika, not believing

how nice Mr. Daniels was to her goofy brother. "Thanks, Mr. Daniels. I told him the Underground Railroad wasn't underground, but he just wouldn't believe me." Malaika reached out to yank on Sammy's stuffed orange cat sticking out from his backpack, but Sammy pulled away and headed for the door ahead of her.

"See you tomorrow, Mr. Daniels. Oh, and Mr. Daniels, you've got chalk dust on your face!" Together the children broke into laughter.

"You two better hurry. Don't miss that bus." Mr. Daniels smiled and shook his head, wiping the dust from his face and bushy mustache. Turning to the windows, he watched as the gray clouds, tinged with green, gathered quickly in the sky. The leaves of the trees that had been turned upside-down and silvery all afternoon, now started to shimmer and dance as the wind began to blow.

"I don't believe you," said Malaika. "You have such a big mouth, yet you wouldn't even ask Mr. Daniels your question. You are something else."

"It wasn't my question. It was yours! And besides, you told me to be quiet. And so I did. So there!" Sammy stuck his tongue out at his sister and darted down the empty school hall. Malaika chased after him.

"Did you see the chalk on his face? Wasn't that funny?" called Malaika to her brother. The children laughed again.

"Quiet down, you two! And walk! Walk!" demanded a teacher, who poked her head out the door of the principal's office. "Either slow down and walk or I will make you go all the way back to your lockers and walk it over again."

"We're going to miss our bus," explained Malaika.

"I don't care if you miss the space shuttle, walk!"

Sammy slowed to a quick walk and Malaika followed. They moved as fast as they could without running. Malaika's books slid around, pinching her arms. Her hand cramped as she squeezed down tight on her ball of string.

Sammy reached the first set of double doors leading outside. He turned and slammed into them, squashing his backpack and stuffed cat. Malaika broke into a trot, trying to beat her brother through the second set of doors. Pushing Sammy aside, she threw open the door and raced out, just in time to see the last school bus pull away from the parking lot.

Sammy purposely rammed into his sister as she stood watching the bus drive away, leaving them stranded.

"Stop pushing me!" she squealed. "Look!" she said, pointing at the bus.

Sammy looked up just in time to see the yellow school bus turn the corner. "Hey wait!" yelled Sammy as he ran along the sidewalk towards the road. "WAIT!"

Sammy jumped up and down, swinging his arms. "Wait! Wait!"

Malaika shook her head. "They can't hear you. We'll just have to walk home."

In defeat Sammy dropped his backpack from his shoulders. "I told you we'd miss the bus. I told you. We'll have to call Mama to come get us now," he added. "She'll be real mad."

"Mama said she is going grocery shopping after work and won't be home until after cartoons are over. So, she's going to be a half-hour late. Don't you remember anything, Sammy?" asked Malaika.

"Well, what are we going to do?"

"What do you think? We are just going to have to walk home," she snapped.

"What?" Sammy dropped his head and flopped down, sitting on top of his backpack. "That's a long way. I don't want to walk all that way."

"Well, neither do I, but if we want to get home

and not worry Mama we better get going. Besides, it's only a little over a mile. It's not far." Malaika walked past her brother who sat on his backpack. I wish I had remembered to bring my backpack to school this morning, she thought to herself as she shifted her armload of heavy books.

Sammy sat pouting. Because of his dumb old sister he now had to walk home.

Just then, thunder growled a warning across the sky. "And now it's going to rain?" Sammy yelled. "How bad can it get?" Quickly he stood, pulling his pack on to his shoulder. Malaika was already half-way down the block, but he ran and soon caught up with her.

"Sammy, we better hurry, so we don't get wet. Can I put my books in your backpack? I'll help carry it."

"No!" shouted Sammy. "Just hurry up and leave me alone. If it weren't for you, we'd be on the bus."

The two trotted along the sidewalk as quickly as they could. They both knew if they didn't get home before their Mama and before it rained, she would be worried and would come out looking for them. Then they would be in real trouble.

Above them, the trees swayed and dark clouds continued to fill the sky. It looked as if the sky would crack open at any second with rain. The streetlights suddenly blinked on.

"Come on! Run!" called Malaika.

Sammy and Malaika started running as fast as they could. Even though home wasn't far off, walking in the dark and the wind made it seem a zillion miles away.

Sammy scooted ahead of Malaika with his stuffed cat jostling back and forth in the backpack as he ran. Malaika tried to keep up, but her books kept sliding around unevenly in her arms. The wind that once made the leaves dance now turned mean and pulled the branches back.

"Come on, Malaika! Hurry! The rain's coming!" yelled Sammy over the noise of the wind.

"I can't. I keep losing my books!" Sammy turned to see his sister struggling with her armload of books. He quickly took off his pack and ran back to help her.

"I'll put the books in my pack. You got to help me carry it though." Malaika, grateful for the help, nodded.

Suddenly, the first drops of rain fell. At first they felt like tiny drops of spit, like when you're standing too close to someone when they talk. Then they began to splat down.

Sammy wrestled with his backpack trying to open it, the stuffed cat staring up stupidly at him.

"Let's get up under that tree. We won't get wet there." Malaika grabbed one of the straps of the backpack, and Sammy grabbed the other as they ran for shelter under a big oak tree.

Dropping the pack against the tree trunk, Sammy fumbled with the snaps on the flap. Finally opening the bag, he jammed Malaika's books into it.

"I'll carry my string," said Malaika.

"You're going to have to. I don't think anything more will fit." Sammy pulled the flap down snug over the books to protect them from the rain. "There!"

The wind blew harder, and the air suddenly felt cold and icy. Above them branches rattled and leaves whipped around in the wind. The rain began to fall in gray sheets all around them.

"I'm cold," Sammy shivered.

"Me too!" Malaika agreed.

Suddenly a low growl of thunder surrounded them. "Sammy, I don't think we should be under this tree. It's a tall tree and really old. It could be blown over or even get hit by lightning. Maybe we should run for it."

"You're crazy. I am staying here," insisted Sammy as he wiped drops of water from his face with his damp sleeve. The overhanging branches of the great oak swayed back and forth above them and blocked some of the rain.

The ugly clouds grumbled again and a silver flash lit the sky near the school. It was followed by another, and yet another. The thunder cracked the air like a whip. Flashes were everywhere.

Malaika wished she were home with her Mama right now. She hugged the ball of braided string tightly to her chest. Somehow it made her feel less afraid. She remembered how a string like it had comforted the slave family in the story her class had read that day.

Malaika was startled from her thoughts by a "bang" that split the sky. The smell of ozone filled the air. The streetlights and the lights of the surrounding houses went black.

Sammy grabbed his sister, "That was close!"

"It hit something. We better run for it!" yelled Malaika.

At that very instant a claw of lightning sliced through the sky, striking at the arms of their sheltering tree.

The two children tried to scramble away as the huge oak creaked and snapped. They looked up to see a large branch falling.

"Look out!"

Chapter 2

The Fire-eater

Climbing the steps of the front porch, Daniel paused and looked back out at the gray sky. Studying the gathering clouds, he thoughtlessly ran his work-dirtied hand across his face and bushy mustache, leaving a streak of dust behind. There be a storm a-brewin', he thought to himself.

His stomach growled in hunger. He knew his unkempt appearance and grubby work clothes wouldn't be acceptable to Fanny, but it wasn't about to keep him from food. He leaned over the edge of the front porch and spat a long brown stream of tobacco juice down onto Fanny's rose bushes. Better than spittin' in the house, he thought. Scraping the mud and manure from his boots, he entered the small house.

"Lordy, did you not find it hot today, Daniel? Why, I'm so hot, I just can't find it in me to stir," drawled a southern voice. Fanny, Daniel's wife, looked up from her lace work and rocked back in her rocking chair, fanning herself with her free hand. She stared up at Daniel and waited for his answer.

Daniel grinned at Fanny, revealing stained teeth that bore tobacco pieces from his last chew.

"Aye, you got that right, woman, but there be a storm a-comin' in. The leaves are flipped all silver-like. A storm will cool the air soon enough. Now, what **vittles** did you fix for me ta eat? Why don't I smell the cookin'?"

"Oh, Daniel, y'all know it's been much too hot for me to cook today. Did you expect me to get that big old stove roaring hot with a fire in its belly? The air has just been so heavy, why, I can hardly draw a breath. I'm about to faint dead away this very minute. Anyhow, there is plenty of leftover cornbread from last evening. Even a bit of salt pork and **okra**."

Daniel's face took on a look of astonishment. No hot food for a working man, he wondered? He tried to keep his temper, but his dirty face began to turn red with anger. Looking away from his wife, he squatted down and rubbed his rough hands over their old yellow cat that lay sprawled out on the rug. The cat welcomed Daniel's attention, rolling over, purring, and showing its soft underbelly. The electricity in the air from the coming storm made the cat's hair snap and spark, sticking up on end.

"You like that, don't you?" Daniel smiled at the cat.

"Now don't be stirring that animal's fur around in the air, Daniel. You know I have an ailment against it."

Daniel tugged at the cat's tail and laughed as it swatted and hissed at him.

"Now stop playing with that critter and go wash. I suppose I'll have to pull something from the cupboard for you to eat, since you won't do it for yourself. And – mercy! Look at you! You need soap and water. There's streaks of dirt all across your face. And it wouldn't hurt you none to take a razor to that face either."

Daniel stood, making his way to the kitchen dry sink. Well, if a wash and a blade will get me some vittles, 'tis worth the effort, he thought.

"Oh, we will be needin' some water from the well, too. I forgot to bring some in before the heat got up," added Fanny. "I've been workin' away all afternoon on this here lace, tryin' to stay cool. Did you see how pretty my lace is?" Fanny held up a small black pillow covered with a white web work, held by pins, with bobbins of thread dangling.

"You forgot ta fetch water?" exclaimed Daniel.

"Woman, what do you do all day? You don't keep a decent house. You don't cook a decent meal. You burn cornbread until it looks like a clinker from the stove. The okra you cook sticks together like glue. Now you don't even bring in the water? What do you do all day woman, 'sides sittin' and **tatting**, making lace for your dresses?" Daniel asked again.

"Not for my dress! You know full well it's been ages since I had a dress good enough for a bit of my lace! This here lace fetches ten cents a yard down at the dry-goods store. It's plenty hard on my hands and eyes earning that ten cents, but we need that cash money.

"Anyway, you should fetch the water yourself," continued Fanny. "You're the one that needs it so bad you smell like an ol' goat."

Daniel yanked his chair out away from the table and sat drumming his fingers. He knew this annoyed Fanny. He watched as she ladled tepid water from the stove reservoir, poked a few sticks of wood into the firebox, and sat the kettle on the back of the stove to heat for his tea.

"I suppose you could use some of my water from the reservoir to wash with. It's just that it's so hard for me to fill once it's used up." Fanny turned and smiled at Daniel, trying to make peace. Her once beautiful face was now sunken from having lost most of her teeth during a fever.

"You know, Daniel, if you were a better man with your purse, I wouldn't have to work as hard as this, making lace all day. I would have more time and energy to prepare you a better meal."

"Oh, now here we go again." Daniel drummed his fingers even louder on the tabletop.

"Why, it's true. My daddy's farm down in Tennessee—his land wasn't half as good as what we've got here, and we lived in grand style."

Daniel slammed his hands down flat on the table. The slap of his hands on the wood sent the cat scurrying under the rocker. "Your **da's** land was a **hardscrabble** farm, worked by the slaves he owned! That wasn't the work of his own hands. 'Twas done by the sweat of others."

"Well, we had corn and tobacco for market every harvest, and he turned a pretty coin for it too. He kept my Mama like a lady is kept. But here in this state. . ."

"What's a-matter with this state?" interrupted Daniel. "Indiana is a good state, and you won't see the likes of a slave 'cause it's illegal. Yer just a **fire-eater**, Fanny, and yer the daughter of fire-eaters."

"My family was very good to our people," protested Fanny. "They were well-fed and well-dressed."

"And well-worked in the fields," Daniel added.

"They liked that work. Their bodies were built for that work and heat. Why – it would have killed Papa to work like that in the fields."

"Aye, so you might understand why me days are so hard, woman. I work this farm alone. I work me own land, and if I hire it done, I pay good cash money for the labor of others.

"It seems ta me, Fanny, that after all these years yer opinion on this matter would have changed. I know that as a child you wouldn't be aware there was anything wrong with slavery. No one said anything against it. You were taught that God approved, and 'twas the right thing. I can make an excuse for yer ignorant upbringing. But now? Woman, use yer senses. You have to see 'tis wrong."

"Daniel, you're just against slavery 'cause of what you an' your da went through in Ireland. Here in America, especially in the South, it's a way of life and always will be."

"Yer right about that. Me and Da saw it hard in Ireland after me ma died. And that's the point, Fanny. Those rich folk in the South with their big plantations are just like the rich landholders in

Ireland. The reason me ma and so many others died in Ireland is that those landholders worked and starved people near to death. Then when the **prattie famine** hit in '48, there was no help for us. Some even ended up living in ditches with bushes for a roof and their families a-starvin'."

"Daniel, the problem in the North is a poor white lives near as bad as some slaves, or even worse. Or haven't you noticed? At least slaves, if they behave themselves and do as they are told, are given food and a roof over their heads. They are property. They are worth something. Any man will protect his own property, you know that."

"Fanny, it shouldn't be that way here. This is America, a free land. Me da and I left Ireland because rich folks were running everything. We came across the ocean ta escape that. But the monster of **submission** is still livin' and a-breathin' right here in America."

"You, Daniel my dear, just don't know what you are talkin' about. Our slaves were like family to us. My **mammy** raised me from the time I was born. She loved me and her work. It weren't like it was in Ireland for your family. Our slaves were happy to be with us." Fanny walked past Daniel, her nose high in the air with her opinions.

"Woman, slavery is slavery, and bondage is bondage, black, white, or otherwise, and it needs be stopped before it ruins this country like it ruined others. It makes healthy men lazy and," Daniel pointed at Fanny, "teaches women 'tis fine not ta cook a decent meal for their man."

Fanny stomped her foot in frustration. "Daniel, if that's the way you feel I'll have not one more word to say to you about the matter."

"'Tis the way I feel. And good – I don't want to hear another word about it. Me da used to say we are all the same. Every man has to eat, sleep, and die. All the same – no difference in people that way. From me own life of meetin' lots of people of all colors I know Da was right – we are all the same. I've seen it proven over and over; eat, sleep, and die."

"Your da was wrong, Daniel. We are not all the same."

"I thought you said you would not speak another word."

"But we aren't all the same," argued Fanny. "And there is nothing wrong with the South. My people have lived there for generations. We are hard-working, God-fearing people."

"Yer right, there is nothin' wrong with the South.

'Tis slavery that's wrong. I knew when you left yer family and followed me north, you thought you could set about changin' me. You thought I'd get a girl to help you with the cookin' and one to help with the cleanin'. Well, here we are all these years later and yer still a fire-eater that can't cook. And I am still me own man, knowing we are all the same; we eat, sleep, and die."

"If you are so disappointed in me, Daniel, why don't you go stay with your **Quaker** friends? Or better yet, go on up Michigan way. Follow your ever-lovin' slave train right to Canada."

"I told you not to talk about that. 'Tis a secret, you know that. And one of these days, I just might go do that. I sure wouldn't miss your cookin'."

Fanny's eyes opened wide in shock that Daniel would speak to her in such a manner. Now was the time for her to take action, time to put Daniel back in his rightful place – tending to his delicate wife like a good husband should.

"Oh! Daniel, I don't feel well. I feel so faint." Fanny stumbled back to her rocking chair and plopped down, careful to move her precious tatting aside before she fell into the chair. Putting her arm to her forehead, she slowly rocked back, waiting for Daniel's sympathy. As she rocked, the chair came down hard on the tip of the old cat's tail. With a wild yowl, the cat bolted from beneath the rocker and between Fanny's legs, tangling in her long skirts. Fanny shrieked and her legs flew up into the air. The cat scrambled away, its fur flying.

"You and your miserable cat! You and your Quakers and their **Society of Friends**. You and your **freedom train**. It will be the death of me yet," she howled.

Daniel had had enough. His stomach still growled and now his nerves were spent. He grabbed his soiled hat from the peg beside the door and jammed it on his head. "I will be back woman, when things around here calms down a bit." Throwing the door open, he dodged the cat which ran out between his feet, also trying to escape the **bedlam**.

The door slammed behind him with a bang as he made his way through the yard. He did not even notice the sky which was now filled with dark clouds, or the air which was oddly damp and heavy.

Chapter 3

A Friend in Need

Daniel walked along the beaten path through his back fields. As he walked he looked at his patchy corn which had been drenched too often from the recent storms. Now another storm was on its way. It would surely do in all that remained of the crop.

Maybe Fanny was right. Maybe he wasn't a good farmer. Some extra hands in his field would be of great help. But he would be hanged before he would use the services of slaves, ever. The indecency of slavery was a horror to his soul. His secret work as an agent and conductor on the Underground Railroad was his true work. It gave him pride, something his very own da would have also been proud of – standing his ground for what was right.

Daniel's stomach growled. He was beyond hungry. The sky above, which was filled with angry gray clouds, echoed back a low growl of thunder. It was only a three-mile walk between his land and his Quaker friends' farm. At Enos's and Olivia's table there was bound to be food, good food.

Daniel walked swiftly along the path until he came to the main wagon trail. It was rutted with use and led directly to the home of his friend. Soon Enos's farm came into view.

Daniel had always admired Enos's stone home, partly because it looked so much like the large manor houses in Ireland. If the house is large, the woman is in charge, he thought to himself. If the barn is large, the man is in charge. But this household was confusing to Daniel. The tall stone house and white barn were both large. Here both man and woman seemed to prosper.

Enos was a man with wealth, and it showed in his fine farm. The fields were green and rich, and he owned the best draft horses in the county. Enos had told Daniel that when he had come here from New York State he'd been able to pay cash money for his land and deed, making it easier for Olivia and him to have a good life.

Daniel stopped and yanked his dirty, sweat-drenched hat from his head as he approached the farmyard. He ran his hands through his damp hair and let the wind take away the moisture. He could smell the rain hanging heavy in the air. I have to wash, he thought, knowing that was the only way he would be welcome at Olivia's table.

Near the gate, inside the **paddock**, stood a wooden tub of water from which the horses drank. Leaves, sprinkled with soot from the chimney and dust from the paddock, floated on top. Pushing the leaves aside, Daniel dunked his head several times. He combed the water through his long hair with his fingers and it spilled across his collar like strings from Fanny's lace. Looking around, he hoped to spot a rag with which to dry his face, but there was none. He rubbed his neck and face and wished he had taken a blade to himself that morning. "'Twill have to do," he grumbled aloud.

Glancing upward at the house, Daniel saw someone standing at the attic window looking down at him. In an instant the curtain dropped shut and the form disappeared. Daniel smiled to himself, knowing someone would be there to feed him. Now if he could only find a rag to dry himself.

Hanging on the line, Daniel spied one of Olivia's colorful quilts. Immediately he recognized the guidepost. It was the sign of a **safe haven**, a message to a friend from a friend.

The bright quilt contained many decorative squares filled with designs of marked trees, roads, and barns; it hung crooked on the clothesline. An edge tucked up under a corner panel, which contained the pattern of a stone house, pointed to the front door of Enos's and Olivia's home. It was a sign that there was activity in the house, and the couple were expecting runaway slaves as guests.

Daniel walked up to the line and dried his face and hair on the quilt. Unsure if the guests had arrived or not, he was careful to leave the quilt lopsided on the line. Even if it rained, the travelers would still need to see the sign, to know it was a safe place of shelter.

With his hat in his hand, Daniel went up to the farmhouse and knocked at the door. At first there was no answer. There seemed to be a hush about the large house. Daniel knocked again, knowing that if there were guests in the house Enos would be cautious to open the door.

"Daniel? Is that thee, Brother?" Daniel turned and from out of the barn came Enos, his snow-white beard hanging nearly to his belt. He was a jolly sort of man, round all over, most likely from Olivia's good cooking.

"Brother Daniel, 'tis no wonderment that thee would come to visit in such a time of need. Are thee hungry?" asked Enos.

Daniel just smiled at his friend.

"Of course, thee are hungry. I know my friend. I

was just greasing an axle on the hay wagon. While carrying my last **load of potatoes** to thy barn I could smell the burn of wood against wood."

"Are you sure that wasn't Fanny's cookin' you were smellin'?" Daniel laughed and slapped his friend across the back.

"Now, Brother Daniel, Fanny is a good woman. Thee shouldn't tease like that."

"'Tis just. . ."

"I know, friend. She was raised in a way contrary to our thinking. That is why we must love her all the more. To help her learn."

Somehow Daniel had never thought of it that way. Maybe someday Fanny would learn and change.

Enos led the way to the kitchen door. "One moment, Brother. The quilt has gone all astray on the line. I wouldn't want one to think that it was hung that way for a reason." Daniel glanced at Enos just in time to catch a wink. "The travelers are already here," whispered Enos.

Enos removed the quilt from the line and carefully folded it. "A good airing was due this quilt. It has been folded away much too long for Olivia's liking. But it is best brought in, just in case the Good Lord sees fit to let it rain." Enos turned and smiled at Daniel, knowing Daniel understood the code talk. Enos was saying it had been too long since he and his wife had an opportunity to help those on the Underground Railroad.

Enos held the colorful quilt in his hand and smiled as he ran his fingers over the stitching. "If thee didn't know better, this quilt could be read like a road map. Each square almost looks like a stop on the trail from the **Ohio River** to the **Detroit River**. Amazing quilt work that woman does. It is a gift for all," Enos said as he admired his wife's work and praised her good heart.

The two men walked to the kitchen door carrying the quilt. After stomping the dirt off their boots, they entered the large kitchen. It was dark and quiet, but the smell of simmering food and freshly baked bread filled the room. "Didn't Olivia find it hot today ta make bread?" asked Daniel.

"Olivia would cook and bake if the Good Lord allowed the sun to shine day and night. That is just the way she is, Brother Daniel. Take a chair, my friend. I will see if I can disturb Olivia from her duties to come join us." Enos walked out of the kitchen leaving Daniel to sample a piece of broken crust from a warm loaf of bread.

That woman makes the best salt-rising bread

in the county, thought Daniel as he ate the crust.

"Would thee like a slice of bread and some butter and stew to go with that snitch of crust, Brother Daniel?" Daniel jerked around quickly. There stood Olivia, as round as her husband and with cheeks as red as Fanny's roses.

"I'm sorry, Olivia. . ."

"I know thee, Daniel. Don't worry. Thee are always welcome to all we have in this house. Thee are a Brother, a true friend of Friends."

"And a good friend at that," added Enos who followed his wife into the kitchen.

"Olivia? Do we have some cold buttermilk in the springhouse? I think cold buttermilk on such a day is in order."

"I will go fetch some, Enos. And butter for the bread. Our little guests are in need of food, too."

Olivia slowly opened the door and peeked out, making sure there was no one about. Then she quickly stepped out and closed the door. In a moment she returned with a frightened look on her face.

"Enos, did thee remove the quilt? It is not on the line."

"Forgive me, Olivia, I forgot to tell thee. It is folded and back in the chest. I supposed it had gotten the airing it needed. No sense waving a **placard** in the **pattyrollers'** faces, now that it has served its purpose."

"So right thee are, husband. It just gave me a start to see it gone. Thee must be mindful of safety." Olivia smiled, and once again left for the springhouse.

"So you have guests, do you?" inquired Daniel. "I thought so when I saw the quilt folded there like that, pointing ta the house. A right trick Olivia has there."

"Yes, Brother. We have two guests this day. They will need to be moving to your barn this evening, if that will please thee."

"Aye, it will please me indeed. Two, only two? Why such a small load when so many need helpin'?"

"This was a **special delivery**, Daniel."

"A special delivery? They must be important guests?"

"Thee might say so, Brother."

"Are they **shepherds**? **Stationmasters**? Are they moving south to cross the Ohio ta bring back more on the **Freedom Road**?"

"No, Daniel, they are not."

"Well, they must be skilled workers then, what could work ten times their weight in the field and have a thousand dollars **cash bounty** on their heads."

Enos grinned and shook his head. "No, Daniel, they are not."

"Well, blast it, Brother Enos, why would anyone take up yer space with only two **parcels** if they weren't as important as all that? You have plenty of room here for an overflow."

Just then Olivia kicked the door open with her boot. In her hands was a bucket of cool buttermilk and under her arm, a crock of butter.

Enos and Daniel both leapt to their feet to help. Daniel bumped into Enos as they both rushed to the door to help. "Brother Daniel, thee must have a powerful hunger. Let me help my wife with the door."

Embarrassed, Daniel explained, "'Twas just that Olivia needed help."

Olivia's face was now bright red and sweat dripped from her **skullcap**. "The Good Lord found fit to let the sun come back out, and now it shines gloriously. Why, I thought we were in for a great storm." She pulled up the edge of her apron and dabbed her face dry.

"Thee are true when thee say that, wife. But thee know the weather can no more be trusted than a rattlesnake. It could turn and strike at any time.

"A mug of cool milk from the springhouse will revive us all." Enos took a ladle and dipped it into the bucket of thick buttery milk. "Daniel? Two ladles of milk for you?"

"Three would be better, Enos," said Daniel with a grin.

"Three it will be."

"Let me get thee a bowl of stew and cut a loaf of bread. I must also make a tray for our guests. They will be hungry when they awake, the poor dears. They traveled all night and will need to move on this evening. That is why it is such a blessing for thee to have arrived when you did."

"Poor dears?" said Daniel, repeating Olivia's words.

"Yes, our guests are little parcels."

"Little parcels? This far north? Surely now, they can't be all alone?"

Olivia interrupted Daniel's questions. "Here now, brother Daniel, is some good thick stew for thee. It will fill thy stomach, and there is more if thee have the need." Olivia placed a large crockery bowl in front of him. It contained enough stew to fill half a kettle.

Olivia lay a cutting board with a loaf of freshly

sliced bread and the crock of butter in front of the two men .

"I thank you, Olivia, for tending to me needs."

"Why, Daniel, thee are our brother. I would do anything that thee asked. And I am sure thee would do anything we asked." Olivia turned away, preparing two small bowls of stew and buttering a pile of bread. "There, they will like this. It will fill their stomachs and make them strong. Oh, mustn't forget the buttermilk. It is so warm up there in that attic."

"Olivia," interrupted Enos. "I am certain Brother Daniel would do any favor that we had a need of. Is that not true, Daniel?"

Between huge bites of bread, Daniel nodded his head. "Aye, I would, Enos."

Daniel now all but swam in his bowl of steaming stew— gulping, slurping, and gnawing like a pig in its slop. He was a man who knew the worth of a good, hot meal.

Enos sliced more bread which Daniel broke into pieces and dropped into his bowl of stew. He ate and ate until he had emptied his bowl, then took another piece of bread and sopped it clean.

Enos ladled out some more buttermilk and sat it before Daniel who grabbed the mug and splashed the thick cold liquid down his throat. Discreetly, he put his big fist to his mouth and belched.

Chapter 4

The Meeting

"Yer a lucky man, Enos, ta be married ta such a good cook as Olivia."

Enos took another drink of his buttermilk. "Thee are right, Brother Daniel. Thee are right."

"So now, tell me about yer parcels in the attic room. Small parcels, you say?"

"Very small, and that is what troubles me."

"When I was looking for a rag ta dry on," said Daniel, "I spied someone lookin' out the attic window. These parcels must be big enough to get into mischief."

"Thee saw them in the window?" Enos asked, surprised. "Thee are right again, Brother. They are just the size for mischief and that is why there is need. I estimate their ages to be around eight and ten."

"Need? Tell me, Enos, why are they traveling alone? Did they flee on their own? You know 'tis dangerous when they flee on their own and find you. That means the route is known."

"No, these were sent by our slave friend, Dealie, from the tobacco plantation along the Tennessee border."

"That Dealie is a smart woman," said Daniel. "'Tis not like her to send small parcels alone on the emancipation car."

"Sister Dealie is a wise woman and has helped many," agreed Enos.

"I heard it said that Dealie would be stayin' on the plantation 'til all her kind had their feet on the road ta freedom."

Enos nodded. "Let us pray that is not a long way off now that we have **Brother Abraham** and the new **Republican Party**. I believe this Abraham Lincoln to be an honest man, to do what is right. But I also fear if he is elected President there will be trouble—brothers against brothers over this issue of slavery."

"Well, Enos, an honest man will shine more in politics than anywhere else. 'Course an honest man is hard to come by, too," chuckled Daniel.

Olivia returned to the kitchen with an empty tray and a smile, her rosy cheeks beaming with pride. "They ate every last drop. The children were so hungry, and they slept so hard. They were playing with the cat and her kittens when I went up there."

Shaking her head, she continued, "For the life of me I can't understand why Dealie sent children without a **pilot** and unsupervised. It is unsafe for them to travel that way. They could get lost, and if they don't keep up the pace, they could miss the next stop. And what if their mother is caught and can't meet them? They will be all alone. I don't like it none a bit."

Olivia put the dirty dishes in the dry sink and poured hot water from the kettle into the basin. She returned the kettle and removed Daniel's bowl. "You ate every last drop, too, and all the bread. It is good when one person does a good deed for another. It makes one's heart shine." Olivia plopped the bowl into the steaming water and washed and rinsed it.

"Now if it please you, Enos," said Daniel, "share with me the story of how these wee ones got on the train ta freedom by themselves. And what is this about meeting their mother? Why is she not with them?"

Just then, Daniel looked down. Nudging his leg was a big female tiger cat, her teats swollen from feeding kittens. "Here you be, ol' mama. Where are yer babies?" Daniel leaned down and rubbed the cat's ears. The cat pushed her head hard against his hand and began to purr. Daniel laughed.

"Wife!" said Enos sharply. Olivia spun around. Surprised at the harshness of Enos's voice, Daniel looked up. There, standing in the kitchen at the bottom of the stairs, stood two children, their eyes wide with alarm at the sight of Daniel.

Olivia rushed to their side, wrapping them in her arms. The older child, a girl, buried her head in Olivia's apron and peeked around at Daniel. A boy hid behind his older sister.

"Oh, my dear children, thee must never leave that attic room without me. It is too dangerous. I thought thee knew that. There are too many people that visit here. It is not safe to wander about."

Tears began to roll down the boy's cheeks.

"It was just the kittens needed their mama," said the girl.

"I know, I know." Olivia stooped and wiped the boy's face and nose with her apron. "But thee just have to be so careful, children."

"But that mama cat left her babies all alone upstairs, and they got scared and were crying for her. I thought she would come if I let her play with my string." The girl held out a ball of multicolored braided string, one end dangling nearly to the floor.

"Oh, child, that cat won't be away from her babies long. Just like thy mother won't be away from thee for very long." Tears again started to roll down the boy's cheeks.

"I want to be with my mama, now," said the girl. Tears filled her eyes, as she looked away defiantly. The boy leaned over into Olivia's apron and began to sob.

"It will be fine, children. It will not be long." Olivia gathered the children to her, hugging them and wiping away the tears that kept coming back. Then she ushered the children back up the stairs to the attic room.

"Brother Enos, I don't understand. Those parcels be much too young for travelin' on their own. I thought Dealie would have had more sense than that. How were they shipped to you?" asked Daniel.

"Dealie's **gunger man** from Kentucky brought them along in the bottom of his wagon, hidden under a false floor beneath the trinkets that he sells. He got them up to the Ohio River where the two brothers, the fishermen, picked them up out of the water and got them across. I heard by way of the **grapevine** that the boy almost drowned waiting to be picked up. The fishermen did not know the parcels were children. They were looking for adults and nearly missed them."

"That blasted gunger! Why did he leave those children alone?"

"Thee can't blame the gunger. He left because the patrollers were already on their trail. He tried to lead them away from the river and away from the children. Anyway, the children are safe now with us. That is all that matters for this moment. It is tomorrow that worries my soul."

"Why were the children sent alone? Why didn't they wait for a full load ta send them?" asked Daniel.

"Ah, it's a tragic story, Brother Daniel. According to the letter, it was urgent. Dealie arranged for them to escape together. Two days before they were to leave, the overseer got word they would be running. He locked the mother in her cabin until he could punish her.

"With her bare hands the mother dug under the dirt floor of the cabin until she could climb out and escape to Canada on her own. She knew she could depend on Dealie, who's family, to send the children on the railroad to freedom. When the overseer and his men discovered the mother was gone, they went after her. And Dealie sent the children on with the gunger man while everyone was out looking for the mother."

Daniel frowned. "'Tis wrong, Brother. That would put Dealie under suspicion. And those wee ones can't travel alone. How could the mother just up and leave them like that?"

"She had no good choice," answered Enos. "Thee knows as well as she that any slave caught trying to run is punished and sold. The mother was headed for the auction block if she stayed, and that would mean separation from her children. She did what she could, and she knew Dealie would make sure the children got their feet on the Freedom Train.

"There are other Friends watching the northwest route through Illinois for the mother. They have been sent instructions to help her up through Wisconsin. In Milwaukee they'll put her aboard a **schooner** to Detroit. As soon as the mother reaches Detroit she will be taken to the Second Baptist Church, a church of free **Negroes**. We hope the children will arrive in Detroit about the same time. Then the family will be reunited and can cross the Detroit River on over to **Heaven**."

"How can you be so sure of the woman's route?"

"Both Dealie and the gunger man think that was where she was headed—to keep the patrollers away from the route Dealie would use for the children.

The gunger composed a letter and gave it to the children in hopes it would help the family reunite. He included code words for the northwest route and the church in Detroit. The children were instructed to present it at each stop. The words were nearly faded away by the time I received it; the water from the Ohio did the dastardly job. That is all the children have, except for that ball of braided string the girl carries. And now the letter is of no good, barely legible."

Enos went to a wooden box on the mantel of the fireplace. Opening it, he brought the faded letter to Daniel. "Can thee read, Daniel?"

"Words? Of course, me mother taught me in Ireland when I was young." Enos spread the letter before him. "Now what is that ball of string you talk of?"

"That is a mystery. The child will not speak of it. Whenever Olivia has asked, the girl bursts into tears. There is also another difficulty: the boy. He has not spoken a word, so the girl tells, since their mother left."

"'Tis the child mute?"

"The sister tells me not. She just said his heart is broken, so his words will not come."

"Those wee ones should not have been sent out

alone, Enos. 'Tisn't right." Daniel picked up the letter and held it to the light. "'Tis a sad tale, indeed."

"Thee are right, my friend. The children cannot travel the rail alone. They need a friend to take them on the train to Midnight."

Daniel continued to read the letter and then, as if he were finally hearing Enos' words, he slowly lowered the paper.

"Oh, no! No, not me! I can't take such wee ones on the route. No, Enos, 'tis asking too much."

"But Brother, thee said thyself that these children cannot travel the rail on their own. A girl by herself and her silent brother? They will be caught for sure and endanger the whole route. They need to be watched over. As thee can read, the gunger thought there was a patrol already out looking for them. The mother is trying to lead them away from her children. She will sacrifice her own life and freedom for their safety. The least we can do is lend our help."

"No, no, no! It cannot be me. I have no experience with children."

"Certainly thee have. Thee were a child once. Did thee never get into a difficult spot and not know what to do about it?" Enos asked.

"Aye, I got myself into many a sticky situation

when I was young. I had ta get myself out of them, too, so me Da didn't take the strap ta me."

"And did thee not ever feel scared or alone?"

"Aye, I remember feeling scared and alone. But Enos, don't be doin' this ta me. I have work back home. Fanny depends on me. You know she is a lazy woman."

"It won't take long, Daniel. Thee will be gone only a few days. That is all, friend. I will take Olivia over to see Fanny and bring her a basket of food. I will bring in water and pull vegetables from the garden. I will tell her thee have gone on a **mercy mission**. Thee will be a friend in need for these children."

"Why don't you take them along yerself?"

"If I were free to go, I would. I have a **venue** for the horses set for the day after tomorrow. I have six of the drafts to sell. There are buyers coming in from all over the county starting tomorrow to view the animals. I must be here. If I had known of the plight of these children, I would have never set out the placards. Now it is too late, and these children must move on immediately.

"Thee saw the child in the window. What if someone else sees them tomorrow or the next day? Someone that might be from the other side of the Ohio?

Thee have been sent for this mission, Daniel. Thee are a blessing to the children and to Olivia and myself."

Olivia quietly entered the room. "I see thee have read the letter. Is it not sad? These poor children are like the children of Israel, crossing the desert alone. Thee will be able to help them, will thee not, Brother?" Olivia looked squarely into Daniel's eyes. "They need thy help. Thee must lead them and be their protector," she added firmly.

Ashamed of having resisted, Daniel finally nodded. "Aye, I will be a-helpin' them, blast it all."

"I knew thee would, Brother Daniel. Thee are a fine man. Didn't we know that Daniel would be the one?" Olivia said to her husband.

"Yes, Olivia, we knew," said Enos with a smile.

"Thee will need to go speak to Fanny about this," Olivia said. "Enos will give you a horse to ride home. The children must travel to thy barn this evening, as we know not when the buyers will start to arrive for the venue. Thee know even our neighbors are not above the bribery of the patrollers."

"No, I'll not go home. 'Twill save time if you and Enos just stop by the house tomorrow and look in on Fanny. Besides, you know she won't understand. No need ta tell her where I've gone, she will know.

Just tell her I will return, so she doesn't worry."

"We know, Daniel. And what thee do in helping these children will forever make a difference. I will prepare the children to leave. And I will also pack a bag of food for your journey."

Daniel took a deep breath, knowing he was setting out on risky business. But getting the children to safety was now up to him.

"Is there anything we can do for the journey?" asked Enos. "Thee knows the route?"

"Know the route? Enos, you know I helped map it out before I even knew you and Olivia. I've been a brakeman in this secret society for a long time, Brother. I just never thought I would be a- travelin' it."

"Thee are a brave man, Brother, and will be in the Lord's keeping along with these children."

Daniel nodded, hoping that was true. How could doing something good for someone else be dangerous? And besides, a few days away from Fanny would make her realize that he was a man of worth.

Olivia came down the stairs with the children close behind. "It will be all right, Malaika. The nice man is thy friend." The girl stood staring directly at Daniel, her hands clutching her ball of braided string. Her brother hid behind her. "This man here is Brother Daniel. He will take thee to thy mother."

"My mama?" asked the girl. "You know where my mama is?" Her brother darted out from behind her, looking as if he had just heard the only words in the world he wanted to hear.

Daniel shook his head. "Best not to have said that, Olivia."

"Well, children, he will take thee to the place where thy mother is supposed to be. That is all I meant."

The boy's face now clouded over again, and the girl hung her head.

"Forgive me, all," said Olivia. " I mis-spoke myself. Daniel, this is Malaika and her brother Samson."

"Pleased ta make yer acquaintance," said Daniel. "Malaika, aye? 'Tis a pretty name. And Samson, just like in the Bible. Samson is a big name for such a little boy."

The children did not look up at Daniel or acknowledge his comments.

"Oh, Brother Daniel, I don't think he is such a little boy. He looks plenty strong to me." Enos smiled at the children who gave no reaction.

Malaika stood before them, her hair neatly braided back in two long braids with bits of pink ribbon on the ends. Her **bodice** and skirt appeared new, something Olivia had made. Samson stood close at her side. His shirt was also new, although a bit large. His pants were of simple cotton, quickly cut down from those that Olivia had on hand.

Just then the cat brushed past them, dragging a tiny kitten by the scruff of its neck.

"Look!" Malaika pointed and laughed. Samson smiled as he followed the cat to her box beside the stove. They all watched as the cat dropped her kitten into the box, washed its face and ears with her long pink tongue, and then disappeared up the stairs for another of her young.

Daniel crouched over the box and watched the children carefully stroke the tiny creature. "This ol' mama cat knows what is safe for her wee ones."

Malaika dangled the end of her string into the box, but the tiny kitten was too little to play and ignored it. Again the mother cat pushed through with another baby in her mouth, depositing it into the warm nest.

"The mama cat might play with yer string," said Daniel. "The babies are too small ta see it yet."

"Upstairs," said Malaika, "she slapped at it and hissed. It was funny. I like kitties. We always had kitties at our cabin. They kept the rats and mice out of the food. Samson, he always had a cat followin' him around, didn't you Samson?"

The boy looked up at his sister and smiled. "Samson don't talk since Mama's been gone. He used to talk all the time. Mama couldn't get him to hush. Now, I think he's just sad. He'll talk when he sees Mama again. Won't ya, Samson?"

Samson smiled when he heard his sister's words and continued to play with the kittens.

"Look at those children, true children of God," said Olivia. "They were brought here for us to help. It will only take a few days of our lives to make a lifetime of difference for them."

Daniel wasn't a sentimental man, but he could feel tears forming in his eyes. He remembered how it was to be a child without a mother.

Chapter 5

Pattyrollers

Olivia packed a large canvas bag with food for the three travelers. She knew it would be a long time before they had another meal, and Daniel had a hearty appetite.

When all was made ready Enos cautiously looked out the kitchen door toward the barn. "It is safe. Let us get the wagon."

Olivia stopped Daniel and handed him the food sack. Daniel grinned from ear to ear, "Thank you kindly, Olivia. It appears we will be eatin' well on this journey of ours, won't we children?" he said as he shook the sack in the direction of Malaika and Samson. Both children backed away from Daniel and clung to each other. They were not anxious to leave their refuge and travel with a stranger.

"I will pray for thy safe keeping," said Olivia. She hugged the children. "Take care and stay out of sight until thee reach Canada. Brother Daniel is a good man and a good friend. He will watch over thee until thee reach safety."

Malaika looked up at the jolly woman and nodded. "Thank you," she said, fighting back her tears.

Samson clung to Olivia as long as he could.
When he finally pulled away fear shown in his
brown eyes.

"Trust Daniel now, son. Do all that he tells thee.
He will watch over thee. Be brave."

Samson nodded. He knew how to be brave.

"Oh, before I forget. . ." Olivia said and raced
from the kitchen. When she returned she brought
a blanket shawl for Malaika and a quilt for Samson.
"Thee will be needing this to keep the cold off in
the north.

"Enos?" she asked. "Will thee loan Brother
Daniel thy hunting jacket? He will be in need if the
weather turns."

"It would be my pleasure. It hangs in the barn.
We shall get it when we pull the hay wagon around.
Come Daniel, thee can lend a hand."

The two men exited the kitchen. Daniel pulled
on his hat as he followed Enos across the yard to
the barn.

"Malaika," said Olivia, "Now do not be afraid,
dear. This route to freedom is well known by this
man. Do you have your ball of string, child?"
Malaika held her braided string out to show Olivia.

Malaika glanced over at her brother, just in time to see him tuck a tiny kitten under the quilt that Olivia had given him. "Samson! You put that kitty back! It's too small to leave its mama."

Olivia wheeled around to see Samson cuddling the tiny creature under the quilt.

"Oh child, I know thee would like to have one, and if they were a little older it would be fine. This kitten is just too small. It still needs its mama. Also, thee are going on a great journey. This kitten would not survive. I know when thee arrive safely to thy new home there will be plenty of kittens for thee to love. It is best now to wait." Olivia took the tiny creature from Samson and placed it back into its box with the other kittens.

Just then Enos's hay wagon rattled from the barn and drew up in front of the house. Peeking out the kitchen window, Malaika decided the two draft horses were the largest she had ever seen. Their legs were longer than she was tall.

"Thee will need to hide up under that load of hay," Olivia instructed the children. "Pull the shawl and quilt up high over thy heads. That way it will keep the hay and dust out of thy face and eyes. It will be warm for thee, but safe. Thee will only be in the wagon about two hours. Enos will take thee near an old abandoned barn that is owned by Brother Daniel. It will be nightfall by then, but thee both will be safe there with Daniel." Olivia lovingly patted Malaika's arm. "It is time to go now, my dears. Oh, Samson. . ." chuckled Olivia.

Malaika turned to see her brother covered from head to toe with the old quilt. Only his eyes were visible.

"Look at thee, all ready to go. Thee are a good boy, Samson.

"Now Malaika, cover thy head. It is time." Malaika pulled the blanket shawl up over her shoulders and head and scooted out the door with her brother to the waiting wagon.

Enos and Daniel jumped down from the springboard and crawled up into the wagon bed loaded with hay. Enos dug down into the hay with a pitchfork. He pulled back layer after layer of hay to make a deep nest for the children to hide in.

"There it be, wee ones — clean, neat, and sweet smellin'. 'Twill cover you from prying eyes. Come aboard," invited Daniel.

Malaika climbed in over the tall mountain of hay, holding tightly to her shawl and ball of string. Samson had trouble getting into the wagon, but refused help from the men. Finally he struggled in by himself and cuddled close to his sister. Enos care-fully covered the children with piles of hay.

"Make sure you can breath in there, aye?" called Daniel. Then he turned to Olivia and said quietly, "I really don't know what ta do with wee ones. I hope I am the right man for this job."

"Thee are, Brother Daniel, thee are. Do not worry," assured Olivia.

Daniel grinned and shook his head thinking what Fanny would say when she learned he was helping children.

Enos tossed the pitchfork in along the side of the wagon to make it look as if they were simply farmers delivering a load of hay to a neighbor.

Climbing aboard, Daniel stuffed the food sack and Enos's hunting jacket under the seat. Enos grabbed the reins and bid good-bye to Olivia. He slapped the backs of the giant horses with the reins. "Let's go! Yah! Yah!" The horses snapped to atten-tion, giving the wagon a quick jerk. They were on their way.

The hay wagon jiggled along the rutted dirt road at a steady pace, but the time passed slowly for the children in their dark cave of hay. Only one soft ray of light filtered in through the air hole. Malaika hoped Samson was all right. He squirmed and wiggled, never seeming to get comfortable, as if he was fighting with something.

In about an hour the wagon was more than half-way to Daniel's abandoned barn. The sky was starting to turn a greenish gray.

"I was hoping for a red sky this evenin' for good weather. This looks like something might blow in. What say you, Enos?"

"I say thee might be right. Is thee barn snug and dry, Brother?"

"'Twill do. 'Tis old, been there for years with no upkeep. Only bought the place for the land and the station stop. Thought maybe there would be a day with money enough ta fix it up proper. The time has not yet come. The place will have ta do, come hail or high water. Just hope the wind don't pick up none and blow with the slant. The whole thing could come a-tumblin' down around us."

"Daniel, thee should not talk like that. It will be fine," assured Enos. He could hear the concern in Daniel's voice and realized the great responsibility his friend had taken upon his shoulders.

"I am mighty glad yer so sure. I hope this weather holds until I get those children there. Oh well," he continued on a brighter note. "'Tis near the end of the week anyhow, and close ta me bath time. A good wash won't hurt me none. 'Tis the children I worry about."

Enos nodded, "Yes, Brother, they are to be worried after. Think of them doing this alone."

"'Twould be a tough road for them, a tough road indeed."

Daniel suddenly stopped talking and listened. He thought he could hear something odd in the distance. Above the sounds of the wagon wheels, there was another sound – pounding hooves beating the ground. Someone was coming!

Both men turned, glancing up over the hay pile. Not twenty **rods** back two horsemen were thundering towards them.

"Stay calm, Brother Daniel. We are farmers delivering a load of hay to a neighbor. Stay calm." Enos kept his horses at a steady pace, neither speeding up nor slowing down.

The horsemen quickly caught up with the wagon. A rider went to each side of the wagon, boxing it in. They pulled their horses back to a slow trot beside Enos and Daniel.

"Howdy. A mighty dirty sky we gots comin' on here this evenin'. I bet you two be hopin' with that load of hay ya won't get caught in a downpour. Where ya goin' with that hay?" said one man in a friendly manner. He was tall and lean and was wearing a long black coat that flapped out behind him as he rode. A wide black hat with a rope of silver **medallions** encircling it was perched on his head.

"Aye, there is truth in those words, stranger. We are deliverin' this hay ta our neighbor what bought it. Don't know if we can make it before the rain sets in," said Daniel cautiously. "How you be finding yerself this evenin'?"

"We be fine. Mighty fine, wouldn't ya say, Zeke?"

The man on the other side of the wagon nodded his head and was silent. He wore a patch over his left eye. His face was streaked with scars and his mouth was sunken in with no visible teeth.

"I do not recognize thee, strangers. Thee are not from these parts?" asked Enos, trying to make casual conversation.

"That's right," responded the man in black. "This here be too far north for our liking. We're on the lookout for a couple runaways, little ones from across the O-hi River. Ya think anyone seen the likes of them around here?"

"Runaways?" repeated Enos. "Hard telling what anyone else sees around here," answered Enos truthfully. His Quaker faith required him to be honest, and he knew if the man asked him where the children were, he would have to tell him. Enos tried to steer the conversation away from himself hoping Daniel would take over.

Just then Daniel interrupted. "Runaway children? Why ever would children want ta run away for, unless of course, they were being mistreated?"

The man with the scarred face spit a dirty brown stream of tobacco juice from his mouth and wiped his lips on his sleeve. "Come on, gentlemen," he said impatiently. "Enough Tom Foolery! I want ta check your wagon for some **baggage**." He bellowed out in a low slur, trying hard to keep his chew in his mouth. He gave his horse a quick kick and pulled out in front of the wagon team, blocking their way. Startled, the huge draft horses pulled back, flaring their nostrils and stomping their feet. "Whoa, whoa," shouted Enos as he pulled the team to a stop.

Perched high on top of his horse, one eye squinting back at them, the toothless man snarled a grin at Enos and Daniel.

"Now what be this? This be a hold-up? A robbery? You be highwaymen?" questioned Daniel, showing anger but not fear. "We got no money. Can't you see we just want ta get our load delivered before the weather breaks? Our neighbor will not be a-wanting a load of wet hay. Tell us what you want and be quick about it." Daniel pulled himself up tall on the springboard to let the two men know he was not intimidated by their actions.

Enos, as a Quaker, was against violence. He sat silently, hoping the men would just go away and leave them alone.

"Now gentlemen, I see no reason to detain you any longer than we have to. But you know there be many an **abolitionist** that live this side of the O-hi," said the man in black. "And we are looking for two runaway slave children that their master wants back. He's offered good cash money to Zeke and me to find them for him. All we wants to do is take a look-see in that wagon of yours. Let's see if you be two of those abolitionist fellas."

"Thee have no right to detain us," said Enos. "We are free men in a free country. This is not legal."

"I don't see no sheriff around to save your hide or stop us," barked the one-eyed man. "Do you?"

"I think it best then," said the man in the black coat, "that you two just crawl down from there before my partner gets himself upset. You see, he's a mean fellow. You know why he's all scarred up like that? 'Cause he got himself into a tangle with a freight train. That one's not even afraid of a freight train. It drug him near a mile before he quit fightin' with it and let go. Now y'all get down from there!"

Enos and Daniel slowly climbed down from the springboard and stood beside the wagon. Enos prayed the children would remain silent and not move.

"You'll not find anything in the wagon except hay," said Daniel as the two men dismounted and joined them.

"We will just have to see about that," said the one-eyed Zeke, hopping into the bed of the wagon. On all fours, he dug around in the stack of hay, running his arms, as deeply as he could into it. He searched mostly through the rear of the wagon, missing the children who were hiding closer to the front.

The man in the black coat remained on the ground, watching over Enos and Daniel with his hands on his hips and his long coat flapping in the breeze. "Ya find anything?" he yelled to the other man.

Zeke stood up. "Ain't nothing I can find with my hands. Maybe this here will help." Reaching to the side of the wagon bed, he pulled out the pitchfork.

Enos lowered his eyes.

Daniel held his breath as Zeke pulled the pitchfork back behind his head, as high as he could and stabbed down deep into the hay with a mighty blow. "Tain't nothin' here. How 'bout here?" He pulled the pitchfork back again.

"I think you must be new ta all this slave catchin' business," said Daniel with a smirk.

"What ya talkin' about? Zeke and me know plenty about the business. Don't we, Zeke?" The man in the black coat laughed loudly and spit ran down the corners of his mouth.

Zeke came down hard again with the pitchfork as he started to make his way forward in the wagon.

"Well, if it were me business, it seems ta me that a slave master wouldn't want his slave picked clean through with a pitchfork. It seems ta me 'twould lessen their value if they couldn't work no more. Would you not think so, Brother Enos?"

Enos took a deep breath and nodded his head, "Yes, Brother Daniel. Yes, I think it would be so."

Zeke pulled the pitchfork back again, high into the air. "Zeke, you be waitin' a minute. What you goin' and doin' there? What if you poked one of them with that thing? Ain't you got no sense? There ain't nothin' in there. Ya already checked with your hands. Come on down," hollered the man on the ground.

Zeke stopped in mid-air and stared down at his partner. His scarred face was red and covered with sweat. "What if they're here and we miss' em? What if they get plum by us and someone else catches them and gets the bounty? What then?"

"Ya went through the wagon, you numbskull, and ya didn't find nothin'. Now get down from there." The man in the black coat stood his ground and stared up at Zeke.

Zeke spat tobacco juice into the clean hay and threw the pitchfork down against the side of the wagon bed. As he turned to jump down, he saw a movement up under the hay.

"Well, lookie here. What have we got?"

The man in the black coat ran to the gate of the wagon and peered in. Daniel and Enos took a deep breath, dreading what would come next.

Zeke dove in the direction of the movement and reached down into the hay with both arms. "There's sumthin' here. Ha, I told ya. Got it!" With one hand he yanked up the old mama cat. "What in tarnation . . .?"

The cat, dangling by the scruff of her neck, hissed and swung her paws at Zeke.

"Shucks. It ain't nothin' but an old mangy cat," called Zeke. "And a mean one at that."

"Give her ta me, you scoundrel," bellowed Daniel, reaching out just in time to catch the cat as the man tossed her through the air. He struggled to hold the cat, which was screeching and twisting with anger and fright.

"She is my wife's cat," said Enos. "As thee can see, she has kittens to feed at home. I have no idea how she got into the wagon." Daniel handed the tiger cat to Enos, who held her tight and tried to calm her.

"Well, are you satisfied, you good for nothin' pair of jack' rascals? You did nothin' but slow our work and frighten an old cat. Now get out of our wagon and be gone."

"Brother Daniel . . ." said Enos with a gleam in his eye, "thee should be mindful of thy temper."

"Aye, I am mindful, Brother Enos." Daniel looked at him and winked.

Zeke jumped down from the bed of the wagon and quickly threw himself onto the saddle of his horse.

"Now gentlemen, we do hope ya ain't takin' no offense against us. We're just doin' a job here."

"No offense!" howled Daniel loudly. "I'll show you

offense." Daniel made his hand into a fist and waved it at the man in the black coat. "Get out of me sight," Daniel yelled as the man frantically tried to mount his horse.

"Scoundrels!" Daniel reached down and grabbed a handful of dried horse dung from the road. As the two men galloped off he flung it through the air, just missing their heads. "Now git!"

Chapter 6

Night Travelers

Enos had managed to calm the old tiger cat. He crawled into the wagon and placed her gently in the hay. "Thee are safe," he whispered to the children. "Those bad men are gone. Keep thy place and we will soon be on our way." Enos patted the hay down. Someone underneath pushed up in the same spot, and he knew the children understood.

Daniel jumped up onto the springboard. He was grinning from ear to ear. "Ha! Did you see 'em run, Enos? Did you see those pattyrollers run?"

"Yes, they thought it best, Brother, unless of course they wanted to be wearing horse patties." The two laughed. Enos slapped the horses' backs with the reins and they were on their way once more.

"That should be the last we see of those jack napes," said Daniel.

"I pray that is so, Brother Daniel. I am sure the children are a bit shaken, but they seem to be fine."

"Did you see the look on that Zeke fellow's face

when he yanked that old cat from out under the hay, hissin' and scratchin'? Was he ever surprised! Now Enos, how do you suppose that blasted cat got in the hay wagon? 'Tis a wonderment."

"I was just grateful it was only the cat he pulled out, Brother. It gave me a fright for a moment. I bet Olivia is wondering where her cat has gotten off to, with all those kittens to feed."

Enos soon directed the wagon off the side of the road. The rolling embankment tossed the wagon back and forth. With calls of "gee" and "haw" he slowly turned the wagon around to face the direction from which they had come.

"Well, there we have it," said Enos. "It is now time for thee and the children to stretch thy legs."

The men went into the back of the wagon and, after carefully moving the cat aside, lifted the hay out of the way until they revealed the children's hiding place. Malaika blinked and shook her head as bits of hay fell away. She stretched her arms and passed the ball of string from hand to hand. Samson pulled the quilt off him and felt the cool evening air. He gave the cat a quick hug good-bye and crawled out of the wagon. The dampness of twilight had begun to settle. Soon it would be dark.

"Quickly children. Thee must move quickly. Now

stay with Brother Daniel. He will show thee the path to follow. It will lead to the barn. It is not a long walk."

The noises of the forest could be heard all around them. To Malaika it seemed as if the tree frogs, crickets, and nightingales were wishing them well on their journey to freedom.

"I am sorry, Daniel, that I cannot go with thee further. But thee know the route like the back of thy hand, I am sure. At the next stop the conductors will tell thee of the arrangements for the train. Travel only when thee feel in thy bones that it is safe.

"Wait! Thee will need the food." Enos dug down in the hay under the springboard and lifted out the heavy bag of food. "I think Olivia has outdone herself this time. Do not forget thy jacket."

The two men shook hands, knowing they would soon be in each other's company again.

"We will look after Fanny until thee return in a few days, Brother."

Daniel said good-bye to Enos and quickly led the children into the sheltering shadows of the forest's edge. Once there, Malaika and Samson watched their Quaker friend pull away. Daniel put on Enos's jacket. It was too big but would keep off the night's chill.

"Are you two all right? We had a scare there, didn't we?" Malaika and Samson nodded silently.

"You should have seen those hooligans that are out lookin' for you. They were all snarly-eyed and mean. But they weren't nothing for the likes of me. I ran them off. Threw horse patties at them, I did." Daniel rolled his lips back into a funny grin. He was very proud of himself.

"I wouldn't pick up no horse poop. That's dirty," commented Malaika.

"'Twas dry with nothin' to it. Too bad it weren't fresh though. That would have got them. Ha!" Daniel chuckled.

"Now listen carefully, children. We will have ta watch it now. We will follow the freedom trail, but we'll do it from the edge of the woods just in case those hooligans come back this way again. A ways up the trail here we will come upon a barn – the jumping off place. 'Tis but an hour's walk from here. We can do some restin' and eatin' there. I don't know about yer innards, but mine are rattling around all hungry like. How 'bout you, Samson?"

Daniel put his finger under the boy's chin and tilted it towards him. "You hungry, boy?"

Samson, with his chin still balancing on Daniel's

finger, nodded his head.

"Well, let's be on our way then." Daniel slung the food sack over his shoulder. Malaika and Samson pulled their covers around them and set off, hand in hand under the protection of the forest's shadows. As they walked, a light breeze began to stir the air, causing the tree limbs above to sway and rustle noisily.

With the noise of the wind hiding his words from any unwelcome ears, Daniel spoke quietly to the children as they walked. He tried to tell them all they might need to know to stay safe on the Underground Railroad. "If you ever get lost, always remember a river bank makes a good road. Do you know there is a train of **safe houses** stretching from here all the way ta Canada?"

"Like Olivia's?" asked Malaika. "That's a safe house?"

"Aye, that be a very safe house. Did the fishermen at the Ohio River tell you ta watch for Olivia's quilt draped on a line with the corners folded to point towards the house? That's a good marker. If you ever see a quilt folded ta point away from a house, 'tis not safe and you need ta hide. Or if you see a white cloth hung from a window, 'tis a warning of danger.

"Watch in wagon yards and **buggy** yards for the **faithful groom**. 'Tis a statue used for a hitching post. If there be a flag or a light in the groom's lantern, 'tis safe. If not – hide.

"As you walk check the backs of all the big trees for marks pointing the way north. And never forget the beacon."

"The **North Star**," interrupted Malaika. "Mama and Dealie told us all about the star."

"'Tis good. You have been taught well. If you remember all these things and stay out of sight, you should be safe and have a chance on this here Underground Railroad.

"There's a song. I'll have ta try ta remember it. 'Tis somethin' about not runnin' the freedom train off the track and ta look for caves and hay mounds, high branches in trees, and empty barns. It helps you remember some of the things I told you."

The darkness deepened and night closed in on the three travelers as they walked the **line**. It became difficult to see the path before them. Daniel walked ahead of the children, pulling back branches and moving aside bushes. Malaika's long skirt kept catching in the brush, tugging at her as she walked.

Samson wrapped himself in his quilt and silently followed as his sister pulled him along by the hand.

The once light breeze was growing brisk.

"Aye, there be a storm a-brewin' again. We need ta pick up the pace a bit. Stay close now. We don't want no one ta get lost in the dark."

Malaika pulled the hem of her skirt up and tucked it up into her waistband, hoping to make the walk easier. Although she tried to hurry, a tired Samson dragged behind, often stumbling over the uneven ground or tripping on gnarled tree roots.

Here and there the tree canopy opened up above them to reveal a sky covered with a gray blanket of clouds. The North Star was nowhere to be seen. The wind had strengthened and now blew relentlessly. The air was so heavy with moisture Malaika found it hard to breathe.

Daniel tried to hide his impatience with the children's speed. He had to keep reminding himself that they were just youngsters who did not know the path and could not walk as fast as he. Still, some vague fear made him want to run.

The children had their own fears. The wind howling through the trees sounded to them like the ghosts Dealie had told them about in stories. Branches cracked and groaned above them. Suddenly the wind turned colder and the temperature dropped.

"Smell the rain, wee ones?" asked Daniel. ""Tisn't so far off. The wind has turned cold. 'Tis blowin' from the North. Folks say that's a good sign. It smells of freedom. Breathe it deep."

Malaika sucked the cool air deep into her lungs. She started to say it smelled like any other air, but remained silent. If it was from the North, she thought, it must be freedom air.

"The barn's just up here a wee bit. We should be fine there. If we hurry we won't get a bath this night after all. And if we do, a little rain won't hurt us any."

Daniel paused, waiting for the children to catch up. As he watched their weaving shadows, he saw Samson disappear into the tall underbrush. He rushed back to the boy's side.

"Samson! Get up!" Malaika called, pulling on his hand. He just sat there. Daniel pulled the food sack from his shoulder and scooped Samson up in his arms. "You all right? You all right? Did you hurt yourself?" There was no answer.

"I think he's just tired," Malaika said. "I'm tired too."

"I know, I know. We are all tired and hungry. 'Tis just a short ways now. Then we can rest and eat.

"Samson? Son? I wish you would just talk ta me. Do you think you can walk?" Samson spoke not a word.

"Blast it. I'll carry the boy. But I'll need help with the food sack. Do you think you can carry the food a bit?"

"I'll try," responded Malaika, "but I can't carry Samson. He's too big for me." Malaika took her ball of braided string and placed it safely inside her bodice and took the heavy food sack.

"Up you go now," said Daniel as he flopped Samson over his shoulder. He reached for Malaika's hand, "Stay close, child. We got ta stay together." Malaika struggled to keep the food sack on her small shoulder and still hang on to Daniel's hand.

"You got ta have cat's eyes ta see in this darkness," complained Daniel. The wind kept growing more forceful. It made him feel uneasy. He hoped the children had not noticed how strong it had become, tearing at their clothes and pushing against them as they turned to start north again. They must hurry. He had hardly finished the thought when a large tree limb came crashing down, its branches reaching out and sweeping Malaika off her feet. For a moment she kept her hold on Daniel's coat, yanking him backwards with Samson still on his shoulder.

Malaika lay still. She seemed to be on top of the food sack. She was unsure what had happened. Then she heard Daniel's voice.

"Where be you? Where be you, child?"

Stunned but unhurt, Malaika worked to free herself from the tangle of branches. "I'm here. I'm all right." She sat up and checked to make sure her ball of string was secure.

Daniel dropped Samson to his feet and helped Malaika up from the ground. Then he grabbed the food sack. "You sure you be all right, child?" asked Daniel again. Samson reached for his sister and clung to her arm.

"Get off me, Samson," she protested. "I'm fine. What was that?"

"A widow maker — a loose tree branch that broke free in the wind. We got ta get out from under these trees, before they all come a-tumblin' down on our heads."

Daniel put the food bag over his shoulder and pulled Samson away from his sister and up close to him. Keeping one hand on Samson's shoulder, Daniel instructed Malaika to hold on to his coat.

With a new sense of urgency they left the woods and hurried into an open meadow. It was then that

Malaika felt the first sprinkles of rain on her face.

"Well, I'm wrong again. I guess we be in for a bath," joked Daniel as he huffed across the field hauling the children along as fast as he could. In the middle of the field they turned onto a smooth path.

Malaika breathed a sigh of relief as they left the tangled forest trail behind them. But her relief soon disappeared when the rain turned hard, stinging her skin. The rain quickly soaked their clothes, weighing them down as they ran along the slippery path. Daniel tried to shelter Samson by pulling the boy's quilt over his head. Malaika held her shawl with one hand and Daniel's coat with the other. She bent her head down to protect her face from the torrents of rain and blindly followed Daniel. Abruptly, Daniel stopped. Malaika bumped into him and looked up in surprise. Just ahead she could see the black outline of a barn.

Chapter 7

Unwelcome Guests

"There it is!" shouted Daniel to the children. "We made it. In a second we will be out of this confounded rain." Daniel scrambled to find the hidden key that would unlock the double doors.

Key in hand, Daniel felt along the door to find the lock. Suddenly he pulled back in surprise. The lock was missing and the doors were ajar! Whispering to the children to stay put, Daniel cautiously pushed the doors open and stepped into the blackness. Feeling his way along the inside wall he searched for his lantern.

Outside in the rain, Samson held onto his sister's arm. Rain ran down their faces and dripped off their soaked clothing.

"Blast . .. Where's that lantern?"

Daniel stepped backward and bumped into someone. He stood still and silent. Then he heard Malaika's whisper, "It's too wet to wait outside."

"The lantern is not to be found," he whispered back. "I don't know where it is. I always hang it on the nail beside the door. And the lock is gone. Somethin's not right here."

As their eyes adjusted to the darkness the outlines of beams and stalls began to appear. The air was strong with the smell of manure and stale wet hay.

Now that he could see better Daniel renewed his search for the lantern. Thinking he may have left it on the workbench, he swept his hand along the bench and rammed it into a pile of tools. "Blast it all!" he shouted in pain. His voice filled the old barn.

Just then a soft hazy ball of light appeared in the hayloft above their heads. The round glow began to weave back and forth. Malaika held her breath, wondering if it could be a ghost. Daniel, his form now visible in the glow of light, quickly turned and raised his finger to his lips for the children to keep quiet. The three stood frozen, silent and afraid as they stared up at the glow of light.

Daniel motioned for the children to creep into a nearby horse stall. Malaika and Samson dashed into the dark stall and startled the horse tied there. The animal snorted and pawed the ground, grumpy at being disturbed. The children flattened themselves against the wall of the stall and moved toward a dark corner, trying to hide in the shadows while avoiding the horse. The barn shuddered as a strong wind gust hit it. Malaika felt as if the wind might tear it apart.

Daniel watched as the orb of light drew closer to the edge of the hayloft. The light danced across the roof beams, making the raindrops which leaked through the roof glisten like diamonds.

Above the children's heads, dirt and pieces of hay started sifting through the cracks in the loft floor, dropping down into the stall. The horse swished its tail and shook its mane whenever debris landed on it. The children huddled together under Malaika's shawl.

Daniel could see a shadowy form carrying his missing lantern. The figure eased its way down the ladder from the hayloft.

"Who's there?" bellowed Daniel in his loudest voice. "What in blazes are you doin' in me barn?"

The children were afraid even to take a breath. The horse snorted at Daniel's sharp voice.

The figure on the ladder stopped and hung silently for a moment.

"Come on down from there now!" demanded Daniel.

Malaika put her arm protectively around

Samson's shoulder. She shook with fear.

"I said come down now," demanded Daniel.

Slowly, a man in a long black coat and big black hat lowered himself one rung at a time. As he stepped to the floor he turned slowly around to face Daniel.

"What? You again? Where's yer partner?" asked Daniel. It was one of the patrollers that had stopped the wagon that evening.

The man in the black coat laughed. "It's you, farmer. Why I thought it was a **haint** or somethin' there for a minute. Zeke, he's on upstairs all tucked up an' sleeping in some nice warm hay. And where's your partner?"

Daniel frowned, wondering what he meant.

"You know, the fellow with the long white beard. Where's he hidin'?" The man spun around in a circle, holding the lantern at arm's length as if searching the darkness. For an instant the light flowed into the stall. The horse twitched its ears. In the next stall another horse whinnied to the man. The children remained crouched and silent.

"What you doin' here? This be me barn. Ain't no one takin' **sanctuary** here 'cept me and mine. What did you do with me lock?"

"Took a rock and knocked it off. Didn't mean no

harm. Just tryin' to get some shelter from the storm, even though this ain't much in the way of shelter. Now where you say your partner be?"

"He turned back, rather than riskin' the hay gettin' wet. I was heading home on the footpath when the weather broke. This be none of yer business anyhow."

The children listened, somewhat relieved to know the glow belonged to a live man with a lantern and not a ghost. Still, he was a pattyroller, and this brought another type of terror. Samson removed the shawl from his head so he could hear more clearly. Malaika squeezed his arm, signaling him to be still. Then she nearly gasped when she felt something brush against her long skirt. It was not the horse. A large round shadow, as big as a small hog, loped past them, skittering out of the stall. The horse snorted loudly and stomped its foot.

Malaika knew that no matter what type of animal had just escaped the stall, she and Samson had to keep quiet so as not to upset the horse more. She was afraid the horse might rear-up and stomp them in fright.

"What's that? Did you see that? Something was in thar where my horse is at." The man in the black coat waved the lantern in the direction of the stall.

Daniel turned quickly as the man headed for the stall. Not knowing what to do, Daniel extended his big foot and tripped the man. Over he flew, face down on the ground. The lantern landed in a pile of fresh manure with a soft plop, and the flame went out.

"Hey!" came a voice from the hayloft. It was Zeke, "What's goin' on down there? Where's the goll darn light?"

Daniel grabbed the lantern out of its fragrant landing spot as the glow of the wick faded away. "Ouch!" complained Daniel. "The blasted thing is hot! And covered in fresh dung."

"What happened?" asked the man. "I tripped over something. Where's the lantern?"

"Aye, you tripped all right and put out the light. I've got the blasted lamp here. Lucky it landed in a pile or the globe would have smashed."

"What's going on down there?" hollered Zeke. "Don't make me come down there in the dark to ya. Answer me!"

"I fell," shouted the man, as he got up off the floor. "That farmer fella's here. It's his barn. We'll be right up."

The children stayed silent in the commotion. The horses paced nervously in their stalls, swishing their tails and pawing at the ground. The children could hear the barn shudder and crack. The timbers overhead made popping noises from the pressure of the wind.

"I've got some **sulfur sticks** over on the workbench someplace," said Daniel, wiping his manure-covered hands on his pants. "I just got to feel around for the jar. Stay put, so I don't go trippin' over yer mangy hide."

Taking the lantern Daniel carefully walked forward, his hand extended out in front of him until he found the barn wall. Feeling his way along, he ran his hand over the shape of an old mule harness. That was hangin' near the workbench he thought. Edging forward he gently bumped into the workbench.

"Hey! Hurry up with that light!" shouted the man. "Thar be somethin' big runnin' around in here. It just moved by me again. I think it's some sort of critter."

A whinny and a snort came from the horse in the other stall.

"Will you be keepin' yer **trap** closed! I am movin' as fast as I can. It be you that put this light out. I can't seem ta find me sulfur sticks."

"Ya good for nothing!" came Zeke's voice from

the hayloft. "I used them to light the lantern," he shouted. "Those **Red Devils** are on the workbench."

Daniel finally found the jar. Carefully releasing the pressure seal he slid the lid off. He pulled one of the matches from the jar and ran it across the rough wood of the table. It didn't light. Again, quicker this time, he struck the match to wood. With a flash and a smell of sulfur, the stick ignited. Daniel lifted the lantern chimney and put the match to the wick. When it blazed up he turned the lever to shorten the wick, and a soft glow lit the barn.

The man in the black coat dusted the dirt, hay, and manure from himself. Putting a hand to his head, he realized his hat had fallen off. Stepping over to the stall he peered in. The horse came close to its master. Samson and Maliaka tried to shrink down into the animal's shadow.

"This be what yer lookin' for?" asked Daniel as he held out the black hat with the silver medallions circling it.

"Thank you, sir. That be a most important article of my person," he said with a smile.

"Bring that light up here, you two, when yar done playin' around down there," shouted Zeke.

"Come on. Let's go up," suggested the man in the black coat. The two men climbed up into the hayloft.

"Seems I have a leaky roof here," said Daniel, hoping he sounded calmer than he felt.

"Did ya ever see what type of critter that was down there? I think that was what I tripped over. It was there one minute, gone the next."

"No tellin' what critters are in this barn. I only come out here once in a while ta check on the place. Bought it for the land. Barn's been empty for a long time."

"Will you two quit flappin' yar lips. Ya sound like a couple ol' school marms the way yar carryin' on. Just bring the light over," Zeke said.

As Daniel carried the light further up into the haymow, he could see Zeke lying in a pile of hay between two streams of water that ran down through the roof. He had his boots off. Daniel could see he wasn't a married man as his socks were covered with dirt and were full of holes. "'Bout time ya get me some light up here," he snarled. "Where's the bearded man?"

"Turned back with the hay. He couldn't risk gettin' it wet," Daniel said as drew near. He noticed the man had removed his eye patch and where there should have been an eye, there was an empty, puckered socket. A chill ran through Daniel at the sight of it.

Down in the stall Malaika put her hand against her bodice to check that her ball of string was still safe. She thought of her mother on the night she had fled. She had pressed half of the braided string into Malaika's hand and told her about the new escape plan. It gave Malaika comfort to remember her mother's eyes and her promise that they would meet later. They would tie the two pieces together and never fear being separated again. Malaika knew they had to make it to freedom. All of them.

In the next stall the horse kept stomping its hooves and moving around. The children heard a chattering sound and a low growl. They wondered what made the noise and wished that they were up in the loft with Daniel and the lantern.

"Ya say this here is your barn?" asked Zeke "Not much of a farmer, I'd say." Daniel cast a mean look at the man.

From outside a low rumble of thunder filled the air, and through the cracks in the walls of the barn they could see lightening flash as the rain pelted in.

"So tell me, ya got any vittles to share with us?" asked the man in the black hat. "We weren't plannin' on staying in this here boarding house so we didn't bring no food."

Daniel had forgotten about the food bag and his own hunger. Down below, the horses began to whinny restlessly.

"I bet that critter is down thar stirrin' up them horses," commented Zeke. "Maybe we could make a meal out of that," he chuckled.

Malaika and Samson stayed in their corner of the stall, hoping the men wouldn't come down to check on the horses. Then they heard a new sound. It sounded like something was being dragged across the floor. It seemed to be coming toward them. Periodically the sound stopped, and there was a low growl and a chatter, then more dragging sounds.

"Food? Aye, I had a food bag with me when I came in," answered Daniel. "You gave me such a stir, I must have dropped it by the door." Daniel had heard the animal below and realized it had their food bag. "I'll take the lantern down and go take a look," he continued.

"I'll go with ya," said the man in the black coat.

"No need ta be doin' that. Sit snug. I'll be right back. Ain't goin' no place in this weather." Daniel made his way toward the edge of the hayloft. He noticed the rain had stopped.

"A strange storm we be havin' this night," commented Daniel. As he climbed down out of the haymow he heard an odd, eerie sound. It was the wind. Daniel had never heard such a howl. It sounded almost like a **cyclone**, like a wild train off its tracks. Daniel hurried down the ladder as fast as he could. The walls of the barn began to shake and quiver.

"Hey! What's that?" the men shouted. "Come back here!" The sound of the rushing wind grew. "Come back!"

The children listened fearfully. All around them they could hear the creaking of timber. The barn's frame started to twist.

"Hey! Come back here!" shouted Zeke again. Daniel could see the two men rush to the edge of the haymow, sensing the danger. The floor of the hayloft shook under their feet.

Daniel ran to the children. The horse reared back in fright. Its black eyes rolled back in its sockets, showing pink. Its front hooves crashed down heavily just in front of the children. Daniel hung the lantern on a nail near the stall and grabbed the animal's rope to calm it. At that instant a large, mean looking raccoon darted out of the stall beside them. The horse snorted and pawed the ground. The children pulled back as far as they could away from the horse's cutting hooves.

"Hurry!" called Daniel, motioning for them to come.

"Blast you, you miserable abolitionist," yelled a voice from above. The men had spotted the children in the lantern's light. Just then the mighty wind caught the doors of the barn and slammed them back and forth, yanking them from their hinges. The doors were sucked out into the darkness. Daniel frantically untied each horse and gave it a slap on the rump to send it galloping out the barn door. The big raccoon followed the horses out as the two men above started to descend the ladder from the hayloft. Suddenly it was still. Then a great whoosh of wind snapped the main roof support of the barn and the ceiling began to crumble.

"Out!" Daniel bellowed. He grabbed the food bag and pushed the children out the barn door. The barn gave another agonized shudder as it caved in on itself. The men on the ladder dropped to the ground and scrambled for safety as the hayloft came crashing to the floor.

Daniel and the children didn't wait to see what happened as they fled for the woods with countless flashes of lightning creating an eerie glow across the landscape.

Chapter Eight

An Underground Rest

The children clung to Daniel while the wind blew them along and the rain poured down. Finally they wrapped their arms around a strong oak tree and just held on. Daniel hoped that no branches would come tumbling down on them. The tree was young and felt to Daniel as if it were made to weather many generations of storms. They held on, wondering if the two men had escaped the barn, wondering if they themselves would escape the storm. Soon the wind and the rain began to lighten. Daniel decided it was time to move on. He lifted the food bag. It was so wet and heavy he knew the contents were ruined. "Only good for raccoons now," he mumbled and tossed it aside.

Too soaked, too hungry, and too exhausted to talk, the three travelers held each other's hands and trudged on in the direction of the next stop. Daniel kept looking back, wondering if the patrollers had made it out of the barn and were following them.

Gradually the rain stopped. The once violent wind now blew gently across the meadow, drying and chilling them at the same time. The clouds drifted away and the moon shone as if there had been no storm. But the improving weather went unnoticed by Daniel and the children as they made their way through the wet grass and slippery mud.

After a while Daniel stopped. "I am sure worn children, and I know you are too." He stooped down and patted them both. "'Tis been an ordeal for us all. And my innards feel like they are nearly touching my backbone, I be so hungry," he chuckled.

Samson smiled, his eyes hardly open and nodded his head in agreement.

"Do you think those men are still after us?" asked Malaika. "I don't like those men."

"Aye, I don't like those men either, child. I don't know. Maybe the wind defeated them. I'd be happy to find their horses, though. 'Course I know that won't happen, since they are probably in the next county by now. I think, if we keep moving, we will soon come ta the next stop. I would say we should be there within an hour or so."

As a breeze swept across the three, Samson pulled his wet quilt around him and shivered.

"At the next stop they will dry us out and get us

warm and fed. 'Tis a station beneath an inn, dug into the ground under the kitchen," Daniel said. He looked up and saw that the stars were bright in the clear sky. "Well, I'll be. . .. Do you see what I see? Look up."

Malaika and Samson looked up and saw the shapes of the two **drinking gourds**, one large, and one small.

"Do you see the drinkin' dippers, children? The constellations, they call 'em."

"There's the North Star," Malaika pointed to the sky. "It's right there."

"You see it there, Samson? 'Tis the bright star on the handle of the smallest dipper. See it, son?"

Samson nodded. He remembered all his Mama and Dealie had told him about following the North Star and wondered if his Mama was following it tonight, too.

"'Tis a good sign, children," commented Daniel. "We best be on our way. We've gone the night without sleep, and I have no idea how close we are ta the mornin' light."

Daniel led them through the wet meadow, following the North Star. They continued to walk for what seemed like forever. Daniel carried Samson for a while, until he could carry him no longer. After he had rested, he offered to carry Malaika, who insisted that she could walk as long as she could see the North Star.

After a while the sky started to turn a pale pink, warning that the sunrise was near. The night travelers quickened their pace. They had to make the next stop before the sun was fully up. Soon they began to see the outlines of farmhouses in the distance and an occasional window lit by a lamp. "It be near milking time," said Daniel. "We must hurry."

As they approached the town Daniel whispered, "We need ta be quiet so as not to stir the dogs."

The three silently crept past frame houses. The road widened and the homes were larger and made of brick. They passed a **whitewashed** church with a steeple rising high into the air. Occasionally a dog would bark, sounding the alarm of a possible intruder. But the three moved quickly, staying as close as they could to the road while remaining out of sight.

At last they hid themselves behind a large barn. Daniel turned to the children and whispered, "We are here. Keep yourselves hidden and I will make sure all is safe. Don't make any noise." Daniel crept away.

The children ducked down and leaned their backs against the barn wall. They were cold, wet, hungry, and exhausted. A dog barked angrily in the distance, but Malaika closed her eyes, too tired to be frightened. Samson rested his head on her shoulder and the two fell instantly asleep.

Malaika awoke when she felt a hand on her shoulder. It was Daniel. "'Tis safe. Follow me. They be waiting."

She shook Samson and the children rose and followed Daniel through a side door of the barn. Inside they could see a lit lantern in a back corner. Around a table strewn with papers sat two men talking quietly.

As they entered the men stood to greet them. "You are welcome and safe here, but we have to hurry since the whole town will be awake soon."

The man doing the talking was very tall and thin with a mustache that curled up on the ends. The other man, although young, was very large and round with bushy sideburns growing down along the side of his face.

"You've done a good thing bringing these children like this, Daniel."

"Well, let's get on with it. We be ready to drop in exhaustion," snapped Daniel.

The two nodded, and the heavier man went to the door and peeked out to be sure no one was coming. He signaled to the other man who picked up and moved the table and chairs. He brushed away the dirt and hay on the floor to reveal a trap door where the table had once stood. Then he reached down and used the point of his knife to pry open the trap door.

Malaika had never seen such a thing. Samson crowded close beside her, not knowing what to think.

"Come on, children," said Daniel. "Follow me. Don't be afraid." The man handed Daniel a lantern and he climbed through the trap door and down a ladder. The children went next, followed by the man from the barn. As soon as they were all off the ladder the trap door closed with a loud slam. Above they heard the table and chairs scrape the floor as they were put back in place.

The group followed a long narrow tunnel, dug out of earth and lined with timber. The lantern cast a bright glow on its dark dirt walls. The tunnel opened into a large, earthen chamber. In the corner of the room was an iron pot which hung over a blazing pine knot which warmed the room. Straw pallets and piles of blankets and quilts lay on the floor. There was nothing pleasant or clean about the place, but it was secret and safe.

"Well, here you have it," the man announced. "It is more than obvious that you all were caught out in the storm. Please make yourselves at home. I know you are tired, so dry yourselves by the fire and get some sleep."

Malaika found it hard to breathe so far under the ground. The air was musty and sooty and carried the odor of unwashed bodies. At the far end of the room another passageway had been cut through the dirt and led away from them.

"My wife will bring food after you sleep. When you are rested, Daniel, we can discuss the arrangements we have made to take you from Indiana across the Ohio border and on up to Detroit."

"The children and myself are mighty thankful for yer help," said Daniel, his shoulders drooping with fatigue. "I think what we need is ta get warm and dry and sleep. We would be grateful though, after a short rest, for food."

"No worry about that. There will be plenty for you when you are ready."

Malaika and Samson stood near the small fire to dry their damp clothes. The heat from the blaze warmed them and made it nearly impossible for them to keep their eyes open.

The mustached man took the lantern and went into the tunnel leading away from the room. They heard him climb a ladder and give two loud raps. After a pause, they heard two more raps. The end of the tunnel filled with light as the man went up through another trap door. Malaika heard the door drop closed, locking them underground.

Daniel took Malaika's shawl and Samson's quilt and draped them over chairs to dry. Samson leaned against Malaika as they warmed their hands. Malaika reached into her bodice and removed the ball of string. It was still very wet. She carefully unwound the ball and held the braided string out to the fire to dry it. "We need to sleep," instructed Daniel. "I want you to take off yer wet boots and socks and anything else still wet and find a pallet and dry blanket and sleep. I myself can never remember bein' so worn. I hope I don't keep you awake with me snorin'."

Malaika smiled at Daniel, knowing she was too exhausted to be kept awake by snoring. She helped Samson remove his wet boots and socks and lay his damp shirt on the seat of a chair. Then she removed her boots and socks and long skirt and layed them out to dry. The children climbed onto a large straw mattress near the fire. Malaika rolled up her ball of string and placed it near her on the floor.

Daniel covered the children with two big quilts and tucked it up under their feet so they would stay warm. Then he picked up their boots and placed them closer to the fire. With the children tucked away Daniel took off Enos's hunting coat and spread it out to dry. After wrapping a quilt around himself he leaned a chair against the wall on its two back legs and sat down to keep watch. Soon all three had fallen into a sound sleep. The only noises in the underground room were Daniel's snores and occasional snaps and pops from the pine fire.

Chapter 9

Albie

When Malaika woke she was hungry. She rubbed her eyes and gave Samson a nudge to move over. Samson groaned and rolled over onto his side. Malaika reached down and lazily felt the floor for her ball of string. It wasn't there. She ran her hand through the straw that covered the floor and then along the edge of the mattress. Sitting up, she pulled the covers from her. The air in the chamber was damp and chilly. Looking around, she noticed that the fire had burned down and cast only a dim light in the room.

Against the wall, balanced on two legs of his chair, sat Daniel, sleeping and snoring. Malaika looked again. Someone squatted beside Daniel and was staring right into his face. Not knowing what to do, Malaika quietly pulled the quilt up over her and lay back down. Who was that strange person? And where was her string? Samson rolled over and flopped his arm on to his sister's head. She jumped and called out in surprise.

Awakened abruptly by Malaika's cry, Samson bolted to his feet. At the same time Daniel gave a loud snort and shifted in his chair. It slid over sideways, throwing him to the floor. The figure that squatted next to Daniel hollered with fright and dashed away into a pile of straw and quilts in the corner.

"What in blue blazes!" Daniel picked himself up off the floor and shook himself awake. Rushing to the children he grabbed Samson and pulled Malaika to her feet. "Are you all right? Are you all right? What happened? Who was that man?"

Samson grabbed up the quilt and threw it up over his head to hide. A shaken Malaika took a deep breath and pointed to the pile of straw and quilts in the corner. "He's there! He was watching you while you were sleeping! He's hiding there."

Jittery from the ordeal, Daniel carefully approached the pile of quilts on the floor. Peeling them back one at a time he discovered a very old, skinny man. The man reached up with his bird-like hand. In it he held Malaika's braided string.

Daniel snatched the string from the man. "Give me that," he said brusquely. He handed the string to Malaika who hugged it close to her and retreated to the other side of the room.

"That's slave string," said the old man. "That made before someone sold. That slave string ta tie your family together. My mama, a long time ago, she gave me her slave string, but I lost it." The old man sat up and gave Daniel a silly grin. "You ain't no slave? Are ya?"

"No, old man, I'm no slave," answered Daniel when he realized the old man was harmless.

"I didn't think you were. I ain't no slave no more myself."

As the man spoke they heard a loud scraping sound from the tunnel leading out of the room. Then came an unpleasant sound of metal rubbing on metal.

"They comin'! They comin'! Hide yourself!" The old man buried himself in the quilts again.

The children did not know what to think. They lay down on their straw mattress and pulled the quilt over themselves, squeezing their eyes shut. The cellar room was as silent as death.

"I've brought food. Everyone wake up. You've have been sleeping for hours."

"Food! Food!" The old man flew out from under his covers and jumped to his feet, nearly running into the big pot which hung over the fire. "Oh. Oh, oh. Don't want to go knocking that over," he laughed to himself.

Malaika peeled back the quilt and watched as the old man laughed and danced a jig around Daniel.

"She's back," he laughed. "She's gonna feed me again. Imagine that. A white woman bringin' food to ol' Albie."

Malaika and Samson stood up. They were hungry too.

"Old man, will you hush?" said Daniel irritably. It had been far too long since he had eaten, Daniel thought to himself.

The woman carefully made her way through the maze of quilts and blankets. She carried a large tray of food. She wasn't old, but she was rounder than Olivia and had a big smile.

"I heard Albie has company down here," said the woman as she set the tray on the small table near the fire. "Welcome.

"Albie? You being nice to these people? Come on now, food all around . . .."

Albie clasped his hands under his chin and winked and grinned at the woman. "Ma'am, you the best cook I ever knowed."

"Oh Albie, you just know how to flatter a woman."

Daniel laughed and shook his head.

"Welcome, welcome, all of you. Come on, I brought plenty of food. You had better get some before Albie eats it all."

The woman turned to Daniel, "My husband told me how you are taking the children to freedom, and how you got caught in the storm. We admire you for your courage to help these young ones. If there is anything you have need of, please make sure we know."

Daniel was surprised by the woman's kindness. "Thank you, ma'am. 'Tis food we are in need of now."

"Well, then eat before it gets cold."

On the tray was roasted chicken, potatoes, carrots, pickles, butter, biscuits with honey, sliced cucumbers, and tomatoes.

"Eat, eat. It's all for you. I will send down some more wood and a lantern."

She smiled and disappeared down a tunnel different from the one they had entered. They heard two knocks, a pause, and two more knocks. A bright light filled the end of the tunnel, then was cut off. Malaika wondered where the tunnel came out. It couldn't be in the barn, she thought. It seemed to head away from the barn.

"See now, that's how you treat these people. They

give you anything you want. Just make a fuss," said Albie.

"But she was nice," said Malaika.

Samson jabbed his sister and gave her a dirty look. He wanted her to leave the old man alone.

"Yeah, they all nice—too nice to me. I don't understand," said the old man.

The four sat around the little table and used their hands to pick over the food. Malaika noticed that Albie, even though he was dirty and unkempt, ate neatly, with his little finger sticking straight up.

Samson watched Malaika as she watched Albie. Catching her eye he frowned and shook his head. Daniel was too busy gulping and slurping his food to notice either Albie or the children.

The food was good and there was plenty for all of them. They drank their fill of water from a dipper in the bucket.

"You know, when I was on the road and in the swamp I near starve to death," said the old man. "I don't want to be hungry no more. I was a houseman. I shouldn't have to live like that—in a swamp.

"When I got out of that there swamp, I ran for ten days and nights. Wore the shoes right off my feet. I suffered greatly with no shelter, exposed to the rain, broiling under the sun. No food or drink.

"Shouldn't be like that for no one. Then I found a barn. Big man let me stay in the barn. I be real sick then. He brought me here."

Malaika wondered if Albie had been in Daniel's barn and if Daniel was the 'big man', but Daniel said nothing and continued to gnaw on a chicken leg.

"I am going to Africa. I told them I want to go to Africa. You ever been there?" Albie asked Daniel.

"No sir, I can't say I have."

"You? Children? You ever been there?" inquired Albie.

"My name is Malaika and this is Samson." Samson looked up and frowned at his sister. His face was greasy with butter from the biscuits. "No we never been to Africa," said Malaika.

"Me neither, but that's as good a place as any to be free. I hear they have a colony for us there in Liberia. They give us farmland and tools to work with, free passage. Everythin' ya need to start a new life. Just have to take the passage across to get there. I want to go to Liberia. Even like the name. Sounds like freedom to me. You know, Liberia—liberty!" The old man cackled with pleasure as he told them of his plans.

"That is, if they ever let me out of this here tomb!" His eyes narrowed and he sat in his nest of quilts and started rocking back and forth.

"Don't trust these folks. You can't trust any of these people," muttered Albie.

Samson stopped eating and looked at his sister. "Quiet there," snapped Daniel. "Yer scarin' the children."

"They ought to be scared." The old man pushed himself to his feet. The light from the fire cast his thin shadow on the wall, making him appear as tall as Enos's horses. Malaika thought he looked like a spider.

The old man drew nearer. His body smelled sour and his breathe even worse. His eyes were bloodshot.

"Old man, move away," Daniel said in a commanding tone. "You smell."

Albie looked surprised to be spoken to in such a way. "You know who you talkin' to, sir? You talkin' to Albie. I be the Massa's valet. I took care of his clothes. I saw to his needs. I used to wear fancy velvet **britches** and gold-stitched jackets. I was to be respected and treated as one of the family. My whole life I do what I want as long as I do what the Massa say. Then one day he ups and dies on me.

"What I suppose to do? I with the Massa since I be a bitsy boy and he be a young man. We together over fifty years and he ups and dies on me. They move me out, sell me in a lot, and put me in the fields. I can't take no fields. I be a houseman. I Massa's valet. So I run. It be the Fourth of July, Independence Day. I lived in the swamps, near starved to death, eatin' grub worms and tree bark."

"You smell like yer from the swamps, man. I asked you to move away from the children."

The old man walked away and sat down in his pile of quilts. "I had a family once. A woman, a daughter. After Massa die they sell them south down the Mississippi to Louisiana. Don't know what happened to them. I try to cut off my woman's finger so she be no good to anyone and could stay with me. I couldn't do it. They sold her off. Sold the girl, too. South to Louisiana. Never gonna see 'em again."

Malaika looked at Daniel. She felt sorry for the old man and wished they had been nicer to him. Daniel looked down, ashamed. Those blasted fire-eaters, he thought. Albie was just old and broken now. Too sick to go any farther except in his dreams.

When they had finished eating Malaika took Samson and sat at the other end of the room. They wanted to be as far away from Albie and his sadness as they could get. Malaika silently rolled and unrolled her braided string. Samson tugged on the end, wrapping it around his fingers. Where was Mama now they wondered.

The scraping sound came from the tunnel again and soon they saw the mustached man. In his arms he carried a few sticks of wood and a lantern.

Daniel stood and cleared the table, putting the empty bowls and dishes on the tray while nibbling on the scraps.

"You gonna let these folks out of here?" said Albie to the man. "They don't let you out once they get you down here, you know," he told Daniel.

"Albie, now you hush," said the tall man. "He don't know what he's saying most of the time. He's been sick. We're trying to get him on his feet to get him on his way. He's just too old and sick, I'm afraid. He might find his freedom right here in this room if he don't get better soon. We had a doctor down here and done everything we can. Don't seem to get no better."

"I'm better, you just won't let me go."

"Albie, go to sleep. I have business here." The man turned to Daniel and shook his head. He put the lantern down on the table and stacked the wood beside the fire. He turned the knob on the lantern, flooding the room with light. Then he pulled out a chair and sat down.

"Now that you've had a chance to rest and eat, we will have to be forwarding you three out as soon as we can. I understand there is a big shipment of parcels coming this way around midnight. It will be best if we can get you on your way before that time, seeing as we will be serving as an **overflow station**.

"That be fine with us. The sooner, the better. Now what are the plans?"

The man pulled a folded piece of paper from his coat pocket. It was a map. "You three will need to get to Michigan in the next few days. We have passage arranged for the children on a liberation vessel. Their way has been set. We have also heard of the mother of these children."

Malaika and Samson ran to the table. Samson hugged his sister and jumped up and down. "Mama? You heard about Mama?" asked Malaika.

The man's curled mustache wiggled high up onto his cheeks when he smiled. "It's nice to give good news," he said, his eyes shining.

"Yes, children, your mother is safe. A friend of mine, Joseph Goodrich, housed her at his inn in

Milton, Wisconsin, some days ago. The inn is similar to this one with an underground chamber. He sent an express, through the stations, to let the children know she is safe. It was brave of her to take such a long journey, trying to keep the bloodhounds off your trail. By now she should be aboard a lumbering schooner, crossing Lake Michigan." The man pointed to the map in front of him. "This is Lake Michigan. She will travel all the way through the straits of Mackinac to Lake Huron and on to Detroit. That is where she will meet up with you."

The children clapped their hands, jumped up and down, and danced around the room. Albie sat in his quilts and clapped his hands, too.

Daniel studied the map. "That is all well and good for the woman, but how do I get these children to her?" he asked. "Children, please. Quiet down."

Malaika and Samson stopped clapping but continued to jump up and down. Then they quietly began to toss the ball of string back and forth between them.

"There will be a **Dearborn** carriage around for you soon. It will take you to the train station, and we will move you out by rail.

"I do want to tell you, **a bad wind blows from the South** today. We have guests here in the inn above you. Two new guests. One wears a long black coat and black hat with a circle of medallions. The other has a puckered eye. The man with the black coat told me about some crazy abolitionist that pulled his barn down on top of them to save two slave children. They're here trying to find their horses so they can search further north. They say they will get the children and the abolitionist if it's the last thing they do."

"Blast it!" said Daniel as he brought his fist down on the table. "I was hoping they weren't hurt, but I wasn't expecting this. 'Twas the wind that blew the old barn down on them. I was hoping they would give up and go home. They are like blood-hounds on the trail of these children.

"Are they still here?"

The man nodded, "In this very inn. As soon as it is nightfall, we will get you out of here. I'm sure they will be sleeping tonight. They look exhausted. They could hardly walk when they got here. Both were limping."

The children overheard the words of the man and stopped their play. Quietly they sat down on their straw mattress and thought about all they had heard.

"Don't worry, you are safe down here," said the man.

"Yes," interrupted Albie, "this is a mighty safe place. The man is right."

Daniel smiled at the old man, knowing he meant well.

"I want you to get the children ready. You see the passage over there? It leads up to the kitchen of the inn. There's a rug and a table over the trap door up there to hide this place. In a bit, my wife will come for you. She'll lead you to the Dearborn carriage. You'll be on your way soon.

"You better get some rest while you can. You will have a busy night ahead." The man stood and shook Daniel's hand. "It's been a pleasure to meet you friend," he said. "The many parcels that have passed along your way speak well of your kindness. Seeing you do this for these children, I know they spoke the truth."

"Thank you for yer help," said Daniel.

The man slapped Daniel on the back and followed the tunnel to the barn exit.

"You heard the man," said Daniel. "We just need ta rest until we are called for." Samson walked over to Daniel who sat in a chair near the fire. Malaika followed. "You should rest, son. We still have a long way ta go." Samson stared down at Daniel. "What Samson? What is it you want? I wish you'd say somethin'. . .."

Samson put his arms around Daniel's shoulders and hugged him hard.

"Hey, hey! What is this?" Daniel chuckled.

Malaika said, "It's just he is real happy to know Mama is safe. And I thank you for helping us." Daniel didn't know what to think. Tears formed in his eyes. He decided it was the best thank you he had ever had.

He shook his head and swallowed hard. "Children..."

"We know," said Malaika, "get some rest." The two ran back to their straw mattress, leaving Daniel wiping his nose on his shirt sleeve.

Albie sat in his nest of quilts, softly chanting to himself. "Liberia" he said over and over. "Liberia."

Not long after they had closed their eyes to rest, they heard someone entering the tunnel. It was the round woman who had brought them the food. As she passed by Albie she reached down and pulled a quilt up around the sleeping man's shoulders. "Poor soul," she sighed. Looking to Daniel and the children she said, "It's time to go."

The children hurried to put on their boots and the rest of their clothes. Daniel picked up Enos's coat and handed Malaika her shawl and Samson his quilt, all of which were now dry. They followed the woman to the end of the passage. At the end of the tunnel was a ladder leading up. Next to the ladder was a basket attached to a rope and pulley. Malaika now understood what had caused the squeaking noise. The woman had used the rope and pulley to lower the food down from the kitchen.

The trap door opened and a dim light shone down on them. The face of the mustached man appeared in the opening. "It's time," he said. "Let's be on our way." The travelers crawled up the ladder and through the hole.

"Good-bye, Albie," whispered Malaika as she left.

Chapter 10

Train to Midnight

Daniel, Malaika, and Samson pulled themselves up through the trapdoor and into the kitchen of the inn. A large fireplace filled one wall and the glow from its flame lit the room. Pots and pans hung all around them. A table sat beside the trapdoor, and a carpet lay rolled up next to it. The man's wife stood watch at the kitchen door, turning to them as she waved good-bye.

"Hurry now," said the tall man.

Daniel and the children followed him across the kitchen to the back door. The man paused, motioning for them to wait as he returned to close the trap door. He rolled the rug back over the trap door and placed the table on top of the rug.

"We have to be careful about everything," he whispered. He opened the back door a crack, peered into the darkness, and then led them out to the yard.

The night air was cool and heavy with the smell of rain. "It's been raining most of the time you've been here. It's stopped now, but still pretty damp," said the man in hushed tones. "Not a night many slavers would want to venture out."

Waiting in the yard was a Dearborn carriage drawn by two horses. Its windows were covered with heavy curtains. When the man opened the door to the carriage Daniel saw a food sack and a jug of fresh water.

"Get in and stay down," the man said. "This coach belongs to a government man here in this town. He loans it for special occasions like this. No one will stop it. You have a ways to go tonight. We want to get you on over to Ohio and up to Michigan as soon as possible.

"At the next stop you will be jumping a freight train on a **surface line** following the **Middle Passage**. That will get you on to Detroit. Then you will go to Canada by boat.

"I also want to warn you. I heard talk that those two men staying here in the inn, the pattyrollers, were trying to buy train tickets this evening. Those two never did find their horses. They said they were heading on up towards the border of Canada at first light. They are going to try to intercept you at the border. It's good you are leaving before them. That there **Midnight Express** should shoot you right

up Michigan-way in no time. The carriage will take
you to the train. Now travel with the angels, folks,"
the man said as he closed the coach door.

The carriage jerked forward, made its way down
the rutted drive of the inn, and rounded the corner
into the street. The driver maintained a normal
speed to avoid drawing attention as they traveled
through the town.

Inside, the carriage had full bench seats covered
with leather and brass buttons. The windows were
hung with heavy drapes to keep out prying eyes.
The driver of the Dearborn was invisible to them,
but they could hear his calls to the horses and the
sharp snaps of his whip.

Daniel smiled and shook his head at the el-
egance of the vehicle. He wondered at the fact that
he was riding in the carriage of a wealthy man. A
government man. An abolitionist. Malaika and
Samson covered themselves with the quilt and sat
quietly on the floor. They were jarred by every pot-
hole and rut in the road.

The ride took nearly half-an-hour. When the
carriage slowed, they could hear the sighing of a
nearby steam engine. Daniel knew they were passing a train depot.

The carriage wobbled down a dark empty alley

near the tracks and came to a stop. There was a quiet rap on the door and a voice whispered through the curtains, "I want you to stay hidden for a few more minutes. I will leave you and take a short walk. After I have gone, you may come out. Bring all your things. Look straight ahead. You will see a boxcar. The door is open. The trainman is watching for you. He is one of us.

"Once you are inside the boxcar the trainman will shut you in and lock it. Be sure you have all your possessions, as it will be impossible for you to get out once the lock has been set. Hide and stay down behind the freight boxes. When the train stops and the door opens you will be on the shores of freedom in Michigan. Someone will be waiting for you at the other end. Good luck to you all."

The mysterious voice was now silent, and they heard the man's heavy footsteps as he walked away into the darkness. After a few moments, Daniel opened the door and looked out. Clouds blocked any light from the moon and stars. It was very dark, and no one was in sight. The three grabbed up their belongings along with the food bag and water and ran from the Dearborn toward the railroad tracks. There stood a lone boxcar with its door wide open.

Samson stopped. He and Malaika had never

seen a boxcar before, let alone traveled on a train.

"Hurry!" whispered Daniel.

Daniel lifted Malaika and Samson into the car and tossed the food bag and water jug up after them. Then he jumped up into the car. As their eyes grew used to the darkness, the travelers could see freight stacked everywhere. They made their way through the maze of boxes to the back of the car. There they found an open space just big enough for them to hide. Someone had left a pile of blankets in the hiding place.

"Here children, hide here," instructed Daniel.

Malaika's heart beat wildly as she crawled into the tiny space. Fearfully she drew her shawl up around her head and shoulders. Samson crawled in close beside her, pulling his quilt over them both. Daniel squatted down and looked out around the boxes to assure himself that they were safe.

Within moments they heard the door slide on its track and slam shut. The boxcar was now pitch black. A man's voice gently called to them from outside the car. "Best of luck folks. This here car is loaded. It's transferring lines from old **Mad River Rail** to Dayton, up to Toledo and **Michigan Central**. This here is the **Freedom Unlimited**! Next stop for you – Michigan!"

"Chain it," came another voice "Chain it good. Don't want no one snoopin' around once it's filled with Michigan freight. Got ta keep the load safe and secure." They heard two raps, a pause, and two more raps on the door of the car. Then came the sounds of a heavy chain being pulled across the wooden door. In a moment all was silent.

Inside the car Samson held tightly to Malaika. It was all happening so fast. They had never set foot off their master's plantation before this week. Now they were on a train to another country and freedom.

The children could hear a distant rolling sound followed by a crash. The sound echoed through the otherwise silent train yard. Then the sounds repeated, stopped, and repeated again.

"What is that?" whispered Malaika.

"'Tis the train. They are makin' up the train. Stay still," said Daniel. The three sat silently listening to the rolling and crashing. It was getting louder and closer. They heard a long low hiss of the steam engine which reminded Samson of the hissing of the mother cat in the hay wagon. There it was again, along with another slam and crash, louder still.

Daniel stood up and looked out a crack in the

slats of the boxcar. But as he stood the rolling sound grew louder and ended in a crash which slammed the boxcar forward and threw him off his feet. He landed in a jumble on top of Malaika and Samson. "Sorry, sorry. You all right, children?" he asked as he picked himself up off them.

Now their boxcar began to roll and slam into other cars. As the cars met they **coupled**, adding boxcar after boxcar to the train.

"We're moving!" called Malaika loudly over the sound of the train.

"Aye, we are on our way now, children." The jerky motion of the car finally ended as it began to snake smoothly along the track. A long whistle from the engine signaled the train's departure from the town and echoed through the night air. Samson thought he had never heard such a lonely sound in all his life.

The boxcar vibrated and swayed back and forth as it clicked away the miles to freedom. Soon Daniel and Samson drifted off to sleep. Malaika rolled her ball of string back-and-forth, back-and-forth in her hands, listening to the sound of the train. After awhile, the rocking of the car relaxed her and she, too, fell asleep.

When she awoke Malaika could see Daniel walking around between the boxes and barrels of freight. Tiny streams of light flooded into the car through the cracks in the walls. She watched as Daniel stooped to look out through a crack.

Malaika carefully crawled over Samson and stood. She needed to stretch her legs after being confined in such a small space for so long. Yawning, she flexed her arms over her head and shook her shoulders. Carefully, she snuck up to Daniel and tapped him on the shoulder. Startled, he jumped.

"You scared me out of my wits, child," he chuckled. "Did you get some sleep?"

Malaika nodded. "You were snorin'," she said. "You always snore?"

Daniel grinned. "Well, I can't say I really know. If I am snorin', I am asleep and can't hear meself."

Malaika thought for a moment and decided that what Daniel said made sense.

"Have you ever seen the world fly?" Daniel asked her.

Malaika scrunched up her face, not knowing what he meant.

"Come here. Take a look. Put yer eye up close ta this crack."

Malaika leaned forward and put her eye close

to the crack. Through it she could see trees and fields, barns and houses, cows and horses whisk by as if they were being blown by the wind. Malaika pulled back in surprise. She could feel the motion and vibration of the train car, but she had no idea they were moving at such great speed. She looked up at Daniel and grinned.

"Now t'ain't that something," he said in amazement, finding another crack to watch out of. "T'ain't that something. . .."

The two watched, entranced by the way the scenery flew by. Malaika held onto a barrel to help her keep her balance as she watched and watched. All of a sudden, she started feeling dizzy. Pulling away she leaned back against a freight box.

Daniel looked over at her. "All right?"

She nodded her head, not wanting Daniel to know. "I'm fine." Malaika's stomach rolled and rumbled and her head felt as if it was going in all directions at the same time. She felt like she might throw-up.

Samson woke and made his way to them. He copied Daniel, peering out a crack. He jumped back in surprise with a big grin on his face. Malaika smiled at him while holding her stomach. "It made me sick," she warned. "Don't look too long."

Samson turned and put his eye back to the crack. He couldn't focus on anything. Everything just kept flying by. It was fun. Daniel noticed Samson and laughed as he watched the boy's head bouncing up and down with the vibration of the train, his eyes darting back and forth.

"'Tis it not a wonderment, Samson? What do you think it would be like to sit on top of this car? All the wind in yer face. You could just watch the world go by."

Samson liked the idea as he thought about the way the wind would whistle around him and how high up he would be. He'd be king of the world.

Malaika returned to their hiding spot and pulled the water jug out of the food sack. She took a few sips, hoping it would help her queasy stomach.

The boxcar rolled on for hours. In some places the train would slow down and even stop. Then the whistle would blow and the train would be on its way again. Each time the car stopped, the three travelers went to their hiding place among the freight and covered themselves with the blankets and quilt in case someone came to the door. The rest of the time, Samson and Malaika walked around or climbed up and sat on the freight boxes. When nighttime came they fell asleep to the clacking of the iron wheels on the track.

The next morning Daniel and the children grew bored and restless. Samson and Malaika tossed the ball of braided string back and forth until Daniel snatched it away from them.

"Hey, that's my string," complained Malaika.

"I just want to see it. Where did it come from?"

"My mama made it," said Malaika as she sat down beside Daniel to tell him the story. "She braided it out of her blanket thread the night before she left us at the cabin. She made a real long braid and cut it in the middle. She took half with her when she left us and promised me that some day real soon we would knot those pieces back together again."

Daniel rolled the ball of string in his hand, thinking about what the children's mother had done for them. She had given them hope, with a ball of braided string. Something to hold on to. Something to tie them together forever. Daniel sighed, thinking about the importance of the string, and also about his own mother. There wasn't anything that she had left to him before she died all those years ago, except of course, the ability to read letters and write his name.

"You and Samson know your letters and how to

write yer names?" he asked.

Malaika shook her head. "Slaves aren't allowed to learn those things. But Dealie knows. She taught Mama how to write her name. Mama's name is Bessie. I used to sit and watch her practice her marks, over and over in the dirt floor of our cabin. Mama said when we are free, we would all learn our letters and numbers, too."

"Aye, that is good. 'Tis important. No one is truly free, no matter where, without knowing how to read and write. Education is true freedom, child. And once you learn something, there is no one in this world that can take it away from you. 'Tis stuck up there in yer noodle forever.

"Maybe I could teach you how ta write yer name. Would you like that?"

The children perked up at the thought of knowing how to write their own names. Samson smiled and nodded his head.

"Now if I have a pencil. . .," Daniel rummaged through his pockets. Finally he grinned and pulled out a pencil. Holding an end of the pencil in each hand, he snapped it in half so they could each have a stubby piece to write with. Then taking his jackknife from his pocket, he sharpened each piece. "There we have it. Now what ta write on?"

Having no paper, Daniel had the children sit on the top of the freight boxes near cracks, so they could see. He wrote the letters of the alphabet one by one, and the children took turns copying them onto the tops of the freight boxes. By the end of the morning they could name the letters of the alphabet. It was time to learn to write their names.

"Malaika," said Daniel, "now there's a pretty name. I'll have ta think about how to write that."

"Mama told me her friend Dealie named me that when I was born. It's an African name. It means 'angel'."

"'Tis nice to have a name that means somethin'. I think Angel would be easier ta spell, though," chuckled Daniel.

Daniel carefully wrote in large letters, M-A-L-A-I-K-A. "That should do it. Now you copy those letters down. That be your name."

Malaika ran her fingers over the markings, tracing them over and over. Then she practiced writing her name until she could make it without looking at the marks Daniel had made. M-A-L-A-I-K-A.

Next it was Samson's turn. He wiggled and squirmed on the freight box, trying to find just the right place to practice his name.

"Samson, that is a great name, son. It is from

the **Good Book**, just like mine. We have something in common, the two of us." Daniel grinned at the boy. "When you get older, don't let people call you Sammy, you hear? Yer name is Samson. People always wanted ta call me Danny, but me ma would see nothing of it. She said, 'Daniel is a brave name, a strong name,' and so is Samson."

Samson nodded even though he secretly liked the sound of Sammy. It was funny.

Samson followed the outline of the letters that Daniel wrote. He repeated it over and over, while Malaika used the clicking rhythm of the train to help her memorize the alphabet. It was almost like singing a song.

Time passed quickly while the children learned. When they grew hungry they ate from the food sack the woman at the inn had packed, but they had to be careful to eat only a little each time. They had no idea when they would have more food and water.

After they ate, Daniel showed the children how to play **cat's cradle** with their braided string. He knotted the ends of the string together and made designs that hung from his rough fingers. Malaika learned to lift the designs from his fingers and put them onto hers. At first Samson always seemed to drop a string, but as they played he finally mastered the string as well as his sister.

Between playing cat's cradle and practicing their letters, the children kept themselves occupied on their long ride. Finally, on the evening of the second night, the train slowed again and stopped. But this time the engine gave a long low hiss and continued without their boxcar. The three travelers listened anxiously as the train moved off into the distance. Finally it was completely quiet.

It was sunset and pink light filtered in through the car. Maybe this was where they were to get off, thought Daniel. He made sure the children had their few belongings together in case they would soon find themselves on the run again.

When the light faded from the car, Daniel left their hiding place and peered out a crack. No one was around. They did not seem to be in a train yard or a depot. His worries increased. Their food and water were nearly gone, and he had hoped this would be the end of the train ride. Had things gone wrong? Had the boxcar been left at the wrong destination? He watched through the cracks, not saying anything to the children.

Night came. Daniel settled back against a barrel in the darkness and wondered what he should do. Suddenly he heard voices outside and saw light from a lantern as it swung back and forth in someone's hands.

"What's this boxcar doing down here?" shouted a gruff voice.

"I don't know," came a response. "I spied it here about an hour ago. That's why I came to get you."

Malaika's and Samson's hearts pounded. They slid under the quilt and blankets to hide. Daniel sat silent and still, waiting for whatever was about to happen next.

The lock and chain on the door rattled. Daniel's muscles tensed. If they did open the door, he would be in full view.

"Well, it's locked up all snug. We need some metal cutters to open this thing up. I guess it will be safe here for the night."

"I suppose. But will there be a train coming down this track tonight? It could slam right into it in the dark if there is and cause a derailment."

"Let me check my board." It was quiet for a moment except for the shuffling of papers. "Don't see nothin' here. Wait! There will be a train comin' this way, a freight train. I bet that's what this car is here for. Here, swing your lantern up so I can check the numbers."

Daniel could see the motion of the lantern as it cast its glow upward on the side of the boxcar. "Yeah, here it is listed. It will be hookin' on up with the Michigan line. I know what this car is doing here. It's movin' on into Midnight."

Daniel sighed with relief. Into Midnight, he thought. They were safe. Daniel knew that Midnight was Underground Railroad talk for the city of Detroit. The men outside, at least one of them, was a conductor on the **Freedom Line**.

On the side of the car they heard rap, rap, pause, and rap, rap, again. The light from the lantern soon disappeared down the track and into the darkness. Daniel made his way back to the children. They were still huddled under the blankets in fright.

"'Tis all right. They were conductors for the Underground Railroad," he whispered. "One of them gave the code word, Midnight, for Detroit."

"The code word?" asked Malaika.

"Detroit is called Midnight and North Star, you know, as it is the last stop in the States on the way to freedom. You should learn the codes, there are lots of names for all the stops. Once you get to Detroit you might hear, 'Glory to God'. That be Windsor and Sandwich, Canada. And 'God be praised', that be Port Stanley." The children giggled at the code words of towns.

"You know," whispered Daniel, seriously. "I can understand why those Canadian towns are so honored with those names. Everyone bein' so thankful ta make it to safety all that way. I'd probably say the same thing if I'd just reached freedom."

The children thought about those places and what it would be like when they would be with their mama in Midnight. Feeling safe again, they dozed off to sleep.

It was still dark when the three were awakened by the sound of a train whistle in the distance and the hissing of a steam engine. The engine sounds grew louder and louder, and suddenly the whistle blew two short blasts. There was a pause, and two more short blasts sounded. By now Malaika recognized the signal and smiled. The train soon bumped up hard to the end of their car, coupling the boxcar to it and jostling the three travelers.

"Hold on," said Daniel as the car rolled backwards a short distance. Then the steam whistle blew one long blast and the car lurched forward. They were on their way again.

When the train stopped again it was the full light of the morning. Daniel peered out through a crack and quickly signaled to the children to be very quiet. Outside there were people everywhere.

Malaika silently pulled together what was left of their food and stood, straightening her skirt. She rolled her precious string back into a ball and tucked it safely away in her bodice. Samson picked up his quilt and folded it neatly. He was ready to see Mama.

Chapter 11

Detroit

Sounds of the train yard surrounded them. There were the snorts and clopping of horses going past, sounds of people walking, men talking as they worked, and even the voices of children.

Daniel stood, tucked in his shirt, and straightened Enos's jacket. Rubbing his hand over his face he realized for the first time how prickly and bristly his beard had grown. He began to think about Fanny. What would she think about his adventure? He wanted to believe that she, too, would have helped the children if she had met them. Fanny was not truly bad. She had just never understood that slavery was a hardship on the soul.

Suddenly the three travelers heard the chain that had locked them in and kept them safe fall from the door. They ducked down and hid behind the freight boxes.

The door slid open with a grinding sound, allowing light to flood into the car. A man hopped up into the car and looked around. Another called up from the train yard. "You see anything?"

"Just a car full of freight, but I'd guess they're in here someplace."

Malaika's eyes grew wide with fear. Was it the two men from the barn? Could it be the pattyrollers?

"You all in here?" called the man inside the car. "I know you are. Come on out. You're in Michigan. You're at the border now."

Malaika glanced at Samson. He was crouched down, half covered by the quilt. Daniel was in front of them, hiding behind a barrel with his back to them. Daniel turned and caught Malaika's eye. He shook his head, indicating they were not to move or speak.

"Come on now. You ain't got nothin' to be afraid of here," said the man.

"Are they in there?" called the voice from outside. "We best hurry. That boat won't wait for long."

The boat? wondered Daniel.

Then they heard rap, rap, pause, rap, rap, beat out on top of a box by the man in the car. Malaika squeezed Samson's hand so he would stay still. She recognized the signal, but was it a trick? Don't move, don't breathe, she thought.

The second man hopped up into the car and pulled the door halfway shut behind him. "It's all right. We are here to help you."

Were they, wondered Daniel, or were they helping the pattyrollers?

The second man tapped out the signal on a box
again. "Come on folks, you got to come out so we
can get you all across the Detroit River. The
children's mother was taken to the church here in
town three nights ago. She's waiting for them there.
If you don't come out, you will miss taking the boat
to Canada with her. I know you're scared, but we
are here to help."

Daniel and the children were uncertain if these
really were conductors on the Underground Railroad. They had come too far to fall into the hands
of the pattyrollers, yet these men knew of the
children's mother.

When Samson heard that his mama was at a
church in that very town, his heart pounded and
tears began to form in his eyes. He wanted to see
her so badly. He just needed to know she was still
alive and safe.

Daniel stood slowly. These men must be friends
of friends. He needed to trust them. "We are here,"
said Daniel as he revealed himself to the men. "We
are here." The children slowly stood and moved to
Daniel's side.

"Welcome, welcome." The man looked directly at the children. "You're safe now. You will need to quickly follow us. We got to get you off this here Freedom Unlimited and on over to the William Lambert's Station at the Second Baptist Church of Detroit. You will be safe there. The preacher will hide you with your mother until it's time to leave for Canada."

Then the man turned to Daniel. "We think we have secured passage for three on ol' Baptiste's steamboat across the Detroit River, but we won't know for sure until we get the children back to the church. Their mother is waiting for them there."

The second man interrupted. "We don't often see white men traveling this line in a boxcar. We have a ticket for you to take the train back to Indiana. It will be leaving within the hour. You will be riding in a coach, not with the freight this time."

Malaika grabbed Daniel's coat sleeve. "You can't go. You can't leave us now. You have got to come meet Mama." Samson grabbed onto Daniel, hugging him tightly.

"Please come with us to meet Mama, please," begged Malaika. Daniel could see she was afraid to have him leave before they were safely with their mother. "You can't leave us now," she begged.

Samson wrapped his arms around Daniel and buried his face in Daniel's coat.

"May I travel to the church with the children?" asked Daniel.

"You'll miss your train if you do. But if you want, I don't see why not. We just thought you would want to be getting back to Indiana as soon as possible. We can change your ticket to a later departure. You can stay with the children if you like."

Malaika's face lit up. "Thank you, Daniel." Samson still clung to Daniel and wouldn't budge. Malaika pulled him away. "He's going with us, Samson. Didn't you hear? He's taking us to meet Mama." Samson smiled up at Daniel.

"Come on, you three. We got to get going. If you miss De Baptiste's boat, you'll have to row to Canada. Now get your belongings and follow close."

Daniel held up his hand to stop the children. "You want these children to walk through this train station in daylight? Are you daft, man? What if they be seen?"

"You are far north now, close to the border and at the last stop on the road to freedom. There are plenty of places to hide you if someone comes snooping around. But most people will pay no never-mind to these here children. It wouldn't hurt though, if the young lady pulled her wrap up around her head until we make it to the church. Most ladies do that to keep the cold off them up here. No one will stop us if we just act natural. The boy should carry his quilt, no sense drawing attention to him by having him all wrapped up."

Daniel was hesitant. He had never heard of such a thing – letting runaways walk about in broad daylight. Were things really this different in Michigan?

"There are free Negroes living and working all over the place. Even this church you are going to is run by **freedmen**. You will be safe."

The other man nearest to the door pulled his watch from his vest pocket and looked at it. "I don't blame you for being uncertain, sir. In your situation I'd feel the same, but time is flying. The steamboat will be leaving soon. You might have missed it already. And we still have to stop and pick up the mother at the church. There is no more time for **lollygaggin'**. If you miss the steamboat, we'll have to make other arrangements to cross you over today." He looked at Daniel. "You need to trust us now."

"Let's go children," said Daniel. "'Tis the end of the line and your mama awaits." Malaika pulled her wrap up around her shoulders and head. Samson bravely carried the quilt. Daniel pulled his coat collar up and followed the man to the door.

"I want you all to walk slow and casual-like," he said to the children. "If you run or if you walk too fast or draw too much attention to yourselves, it tells everyone you have a secret. People here won't bother you, but I have never heard of a snitch turning down a bribe from a pattyroller if they have seen something suspicious. And if they have any bounty men out here lookin' for you, there might be trouble."

Samson reached for Malaika's hand as he remembered the men from the barn.

"Let's move," said the man with the watch. He slid open the door and hopped out of the boxcar onto the ground. The second man hopped down and started walking from the car. The watchman popped his head back into the car and motioned to them. "It's clear, come on."

Daniel slowly edged his way to the side of the opening and lowered himself to the ground. Samson and Malaika followed. The bright light made Malaika see spots for a moment. When her vision cleared she could see heavy clouds in the sky and trees swaying in a light wind.

She realized as she looked around that they were not at the main depot but down the tracks a long way from the engine. All sorts of people were around, especially workmen loading and unloading freight cars and wagons. Malaika held her wrap around her head with one hand and hung on tight to her brother's hand. Daniel walked close to them while one of the 'conductors' led the group and the other walked behind them.

Malaika was surprised at the number of Negro men who were at work moving the freight to and from the train. Occasionally one would look in their direction and smile. She wondered if they knew she and Samson were taking the last steps on the way to freedom.

The man leading the group stopped. "Wait here," he instructed. He walked up to a man who was sitting in a wagon that was being loaded with barrels. The two spoke as if they knew each other. Soon the man with the watch motioned for Daniel and the children to climb aboard the wagon.

"Looks like he got you a ride. Come on," said his partner who was following behind them.

"Here you are," said the first man as he waved for them to come over to the back of the wagon. "Climb on up. Keep your heads down."

The wagon was an open farm wagon, just a **buckboard** with no canvas covering. When they climbed into the wagon they discovered a space had been left in the middle for them to hide among the barrels.

"You are only going a couple miles up the road. This wagon will be just fine for you. The driver will drop you off at the church. Someone will be waiting there for you."

The man from the train closed the wagon's tailgate and waved. "Take care now."

"Haw, haw!" shouted the driver. The wagon started forward with a jerk as the horses pulled their heavy load. They traveled along a muddy road which ran beside the train tracks. Soon the wagon approached the depot. Samson crouched in fear while Malaika peeked around the barrels in curiosity. Daniel looked out over the barrels, watching to make sure all was safe.

Malaika was amazed by what she saw. There were ladies with parasols, children running and playing, and men dressed up in their fine clothes. Negro people were there, too! She was surprised to see one talking with the white people. He did not act like a slave or servant. Malaika took a deep breath and smiled. This was sure a strange and wonderful place!

Suddenly Daniel ducked down. He motioned for the children to do the same. Something was wrong! Malaika pulled her wrap over their heads.

The wagon continued past the boardwalk, never changing its slow pace. Malaika peeked out. At the end of the boardwalk stood the two patrollers from the barn. They looked as proud and mean as ever. Her eyes froze on them as the wagon moved closer and closer.

The patrollers were watching passengers get off the trains. They looked tired and dirty. The man with the puckered eye now wore a red bandana wrapped around his head and across his bad eye. He carried a walking stick. The tall man still wore his long black coat and black hat with silver medallions, but the hat was covered with splats of dried mud. The patrollers stared at everyone that passed by them.

Daniel knew that even though they were in Michigan, the children were still outlaws according to the **Fugitive Slave Law**. They still could be sent back to their owner. They needed to be very careful, at least for one more day.

As their wagon bumped and jostled past the men, it splashed mud up onto the boardwalk and onto the men's boots. "Hey! Watch it!" yelled the man in the black coat as he shook his fist in the air towards their driver. Daniel smiled to himself.

The wagon changed directions and pulled away from the train station and on to a **cobblestone** street. The horse's shoes clicked on the stones as it walked. Daniel and the children continued to stay low in the wagon so that they would not be seen.

After traveling several blocks along the paved street the driver cleared his throat and called out to the horses in a sharp voice. "Whoa, Whoa." The wagon stopped and the driver called out loudly, "Delivery!" The driver glanced back over his shoulder at his passengers. "All right, folks, you're here. It's safe to come out."

Just then the wagon's tailgate was opened by a Negro man in a neat suit of clothes. "Welcome," he said, "I am William Lambert. Come along. No time to waste." He peered into the wagon and smiled at Daniel. "All is clear, friend. You must be the white man that we were told would bring the children to us. Come on now, don't be afraid. Where are the children?"

Malaika pulled the shawl from their heads and the children sat up slowly. The three crawled awkwardly out of the wagon, stiff from their crouched positions. William Lambert closed the tailgate and the wagon pulled away, leaving them standing in the street.

"Thank you, brother, for the delivery," called Reverend Lambert after the wagon.

Samson saw the wagon driver lift his hand up over his head and wave a farewell to them.

"Come now, follow me," said Reverend Lambert.

"Is our mama here?" asked Malaika.

The man did not answer and continued to lead the way. Samson, not hearing a response, pulled back on his sister's arm. Daniel could see his confusion and put his arm around Samson, urging him off the street.

In front of them stood a large brick church. The man led them into the church and down steps into a tiny basement room. In the room was a table with some bread, water, and apples.

"You folks make yourselves comfortable. Get a bite to eat. I hear they will be moving you out soon."

"Sir?" asked Daniel, "Where is the mother of these children? Is she not here? We were told she would be here waiting for them. They are all to leave for Canada together." Malaika and Samson stood close to Daniel, waiting for the answer.

The man looked down and hesitated, knowing

how disappointed the children were going to be to hear his news. "Yes, the children's mother – she was here. Here for three days. We got word this morning there were bounty men here from Kentucky looking for her and the children. When you didn't arrive in time to catch De Baptiste's steamboat, we thought it best to move her across anyway. It was for her own safety. She cried. She did not want to leave for Canada without the children."

"You say she was here. She is safe then?" asked Daniel for the children's benefit.

"Yes, safe indeed. De Baptiste's boat would have left the dock crossing over to Canada not more than a quarter-of-an-hour ago. We couldn't take the chance to wait any longer.

"In Canada people from the First Baptist Church in Sandwich will meet her and take her to **Slave Haven**. They have a place for her and the children to stay. She is a free woman now, just like these children will be in a short time.

"Since you missed the steamboat some of our brothers made arrangements with a man that will sail the children across the Detroit River. We just need to wait for the final word to know all is ready for them. It will come soon.

"And, sir, as soon as the children go, you should

leave for the train station. There will be a ticket waiting for you there."

Samson flopped down in a chair and drew his arms across his chest. He was angry. Angry tears burned his cheeks. When would he see Mama?

The man left the tiny basement room and closed the door behind him.

Malaika put her arm around Samson. "You heard what the man said. Mama is free. She is free, Samson, just like we dreamed. Just like Dealie said, and soon we will be free, too."

Chapter 12

Escape

Daniel stooped down and put his arms around the children. He knew how disappointed they were. "I know you are disappointed. I am disappointed, too. I won't get a chance to meet your mama, but you both will be with her real soon. She is waiting for you, just across the river where 'tis safe. When you are all back together again Malaika can sit and knot the string back together.

"You still got the ball of string, don't you?" asked Daniel.

Malaika patted the place where the string was hidden and nodded.

"And Samson, I bet your Mama will find you a nice cat to play with, too." Samson knew Daniel was right, but it still hurt him to think that Mama wasn't there waiting for him. He wiped his tears on his sleeve and nodded his head.

Malaika smiled at the thought of them all together in Canada, tying their string together forever. Freedom, freedom at last. It was their dream.

"I got real scared when I saw those pattyrollers at the station," said Malaika. "Didn't you?" she questioned Daniel.

"Aye, well, those old mangy rascals will never get their hands on the likes of you two, I'll see to that – I promise. But we will still have to be careful until we get you over to the other side. They could be snooping around any place.

"Did you see how mad that one fellow got when the wagon splashed mud on his boots?" Daniel laughed.

"That will show 'em!" Malaika giggled.

The three sat quietly and ate the apples and bread. It was hard to wait for word about the trip across the river. Daniel paced impatiently in the tiny room. He knew he had done the right thing by coming with the children to the church. They still needed him on their journey to freedom.

As he paced Daniel noticed marks and scribbles on the walls of the room. They had been left by slaves who had passed this way to freedom. Daniel scanned the walls and read the names to himself. He was happy to see so many slaves could write their names and that so many had traveled through the line.

"If we hadn't worn out the pencils, children, you

could write your names up here on this wall, too," said Daniel. "Just think of it, children", he said, pointing at the walls. "These are all people who came here on their way to freedom. I wonder what the old fire-eaters would have to say about all this?"

Daniel started reading the names aloud. He stopped when he saw the name 'Bessie'. It was the children's mama!

Daniel grabbed Samson's hand and led him to the marks. With a wide grin Daniel teased, "Well, lookie here. That be someone special?"

Malaika got up and looked at the spot. Instantly she saw her mother's name. "Mama! Mama! Those are Mama's marks. It says Bessie! Look Samson, it's Mama's marks. She really was here. She really was waiting for us. She really is safe!" The two children grabbed each other's arms and jumped up and down.

"That does it, children. We have to put your names there with Bessie's name. 'Twas meant to be." Daniel pulled out his jackknife. "This will have to do," he said as he held Malaika's hand to help her scratch her letters into the wall beside Bessie's name. Malaika brushed away the plaster dust and smiled as she made her letters.

Samson carefully and neatly scratched his name

on the wall.

"Look children, you are all three together again here on this wall. You will all be together again in Canada soon."

Samson silently stared at the wall, seeing their names written together for the first time. He turned and looked at Daniel, his face glowing, and in a raspy voice said, "Thank you, Daniel."

Shocked, Daniel gulped, fighting back tears. "Why, you be welcome, son."

Malaika threw her arms around her brother. "You are talking! You are talking again!"

At the door there was a sudden knock. Reverend Lambert opened the door and popped his head in. "Children, we got a buggy waiting outside for you. You must leave now.

"Sir," he said to Daniel, "your train ticket is waiting for you at the depot."

Samson and Malaika grabbed onto Daniel's hand. "Please come with us — at least to the boat," insisted Malaika.

"Please, Daniel," chimed Samson. "What if those bad men come back?"

Daniel picked up Malaika's wrap. "Malaika, you got the string?" he asked.

"Yes," Malaika said.

"Then what are we waiting for?" Daniel needed to see the children safely to the river, even if he had to walk back to Indiana.

Reverend Lambert shook Daniel's hand. "You are a good man, Daniel, and brave. Godspeed to all of you now across that River Jordan to the **Promised Land**. Arrangements have been secured on a small freighting boat. This sailor has taken many to their freedom across the Jordan River."

"Jordan River?" asked Samson. "I thought we were going across the Detroit River."

Daniel and the preacher laughed.

"They are just talking code again, Samson," assured Malaika. "Let's go see Mama."

The three made their way up the steps and into the street where they climbed into a small black buggy. It was a tight fit. The buggy was built for two, not three. A man sat on a high seat in front of them. He tickled the back of his bay-colored horse with a long black buggy whip, and the horse began to trot down the cobblestone street. They turned to look back at the preacher who still stood in the street. While they watched another wagon pulled up and stopped beside the church.

"Looks like another delivery," commented Daniel.

The sky was filled with dark gray clouds and a cool Canadian wind blew on them as the buggy made its way down the street. Soon it turned down an alley that led past large old warehouses with boxes and barrels of freight stacked outside. Malaika wondered what had happened to the boxes they had written on in the boxcar. Surely someone somewhere would see her name.

The buggy soon turned down a dirt road. Mud and water splashed them as the buggy plunged into puddle after puddle. There were no buildings to protect them from the brisk wind, and Samson shivered. The horse snorted and struggled against the wind.

"Don't like the looks of those clouds. Dirty sky means rain. Can't sail in a small vessel across open water in this weather," a worried Daniel muttered to himself.

Soon the buggy made another turn and before them they could see the wide river. The trees that dotted the riverbank blew wildly in the wind as the buggy left the road and made its way along a narrow winding path. At the end of the path a man stood waving to them. As soon as he knew the driver had seen him, he disappeared down the river embankment.

The carriage stopped. "There you are, folks," said the driver looking back. He was a young man with a big smile. "That's Canada across there," he said, pointing out towards the water. He looked at Daniel. "Sir, I will wait for you to get the children on the boat and take you to the train."

"Thank you," responded Daniel, "but it might take a minute."

"I will wait until you tell me not to. Safe passage, children, and good luck in Sandwich. I took your mother to the steamer this morning. She is anxious to see you both. When you get over on the other side the first house you see will have drinking gourds hung by the door. That is where you will find your mother."

"Drinking gourds?" questioned Samson.

"Drinking gourds, silly," answered Malaika sharply, "like the Little Dipper and the North Star. Gourds!

"Thank you," Malaika said more politely to the driver as the three stepped down from the buggy while staring across the water to Canada.

Daniel led the way up over the knoll and down the embankment to the water's edge. A large rowboat was there, resting on logs. A mast with a sail wrapped around it rose from the bow of the boat.

the man with rolled-up sleeves and pants stood waiting.

"This way," he called over the sound of the waves as they slapped against the shore. "The wind is up, but I think we might be able to sail once we have cleared the weeds along the shore. You will have to give me a hand getting the boat out."

"'Twill be my pleasure," responded Daniel. "The water looks pretty rough to be takin' these children out, though."

"Yes, but the arrangements have been made. I must get these children across now. There are men looking for them. It is not safe for them to hide in Detroit any longer.

"Come on, children. Climb aboard. The waves are high, but this is a good boat. She can take it. Just remember you are going to freedom."

The man looked at Daniel. "You ever rowed a boat before?"

"Row a boat? But I'm not crossin' with the children," said Daniel in confusion.

"Well, if you want to get them to safety, you'll be crossin' with 'em. There goes your buggy, and it looks to me like there are some unexpected visitors coming."

Daniel and the children turned just in time to

see their buggy fly up the narrow path back to th
road. It was trying to block a wagon carrying two
men.

"Hurry. Into the boat, children," instructed the
man. He turned to Daniel. "The water is choppy.
Rowing will be hard, but it's only a mile across.
You'll be an expert before we get there.

"Young lady, sit on the middle bench. Just hold
on. Don't be afraid," he told Malaika.

"Sir, you sit in the back here where there's leg
room. You will be taking those oars in your hands.
Grab them hard and hold on to them. We will be
sunk if one of them gets away from you."

The man bunched his hands into a tight ball,
showing Daniel how to grip the oars. His strong
arms and thick wrists showed that he had made
this trip many times.

Daniel put his hands out, imitating the man.

"You look strong enough. Must be a good farmer.
Today you'll make a good oarsman for these children. Now listen. You must pull the oars evenly with
both hands or you will turn the boat. Keep your
feet out in front of you because the oars will pull
you back if they get the chance. Now, push your
hands forward." The man demonstrated the movement for Daniel.

"The oars will go out behind you. Pull them up and dip the oars back into the water. Once they're in the water you will feel the pull. You pull back and cut down to make a circle. The oars will start to sing in their sockets. You'll hear the rhythm. You'll need to keep up with me. They should click in the sockets at the same beat. We're gonna be pulling about a half-hour with this wind. Then I'll let the sheet out. We will fly across with the sail.

"Any questions?"

Daniel shook his head. "No, I can do it."

"Good. We better be on our way then. You children sit down and hold on. Don't stand until we are safely aground on the other side."

Malaika and Samson scrambled aboard.

"Help me push the bow out into the water and then crawl in," the sailor instructed Daniel. "I'll push it out away from shore.

"Young lady," he called to Malaika, "hand me that rope in the front there."

Malaika reached forward and picked up a coiled rope, one end of which was tied to the bow. Struggling to remain seated and to keep the rope coiled, Malaika tossed it back to the man.

"I got it," shouted the sailor. He and Daniel pushed the boat off its **rollers** and into the water.

The bow caught a wave and rose up suddenly. Malaika and Samson held on tight to the plank seat.

"Get in," yelled the man to Daniel who was standing ankle deep in the water and holding the side of the boat. Daniel hopped in and took his place.

"Don't put the oars in the water yet, but be ready," the man called. Keeping hold of the line which was tied to the bow, the man pushed the boat further out and climbed in. He called back to Daniel. "Put your oars in the water and be ready to pull."

As he took his seat in the boat the sailor glanced up. "Oh, oh! Here comes your company." The sailor quickly put his oars into the water and yelled to Daniel to pull. As they pulled they could see the wagon pulling past the buggy and charging down the path at breakneck speed. The buggy turned and chased after the wagon, the driver of the buggy snapping his whip in the air at the men in the wagon.

"Row hard!" cried the sailor as he and Daniel forced the boat through the waves and away from shore.

By now the wagon had reached the bank and halted. The children could see the two men, one with a long, black coat and black hat encircled with silver medallions, the other carrying a cane and with a red bandanna wrapped around his head. The men jumped from the wagon and raced to the river, shouting and screaming, waving their fists in the air, and jumping up and down in the shallow water. It was the pattyrollers! Still coming behind them was the driver of the buggy with his whip.

Daniel and the man set their backs into their task. The oars cut and pulled, cut and pulled at the water. As they worked they watched the man with the puckered eye swinging his cane high into the air and calling out after them. The man in the black coat took out a gun and began shooting into the air, demanding that the children be returned.

Just then the driver of the buggy reached the bank and jumped to the ground, his whip in hand. Taking careful aim he swung the whip, snapping the gun out of the patroller's hand.

The children watched and cheered, while Daniel and the sailor took a moment to catch their breath. Above the wind they could hear the men shouting and hollering, blaming each other for letting their reward money move out into the river and out of reach. Daniel and the sailor began rowing again, while the children watched the pattyrollers until they were nothing more than dots along the shore.

Chapter 13

Homeward Bound

The cold wind and waves pushed hard against the boat, forcing Daniel and the sailor to pull on their oars with all their strength. From the Canadian side of the river the sound of thunder now rumbled across the water toward them. Frightened by the bobbing motion of the boat, the wind, and now by the threat of a storm, Malaika and Samson clutched the wooden seats so tightly their hands ached.

"I think the wind is shifting," the sailor shouted to Daniel. "Keep pulling and if the wind steadies, I think I'll be able to put up the sail." The man dropped his oars into the boat and carefully made his way to a mast in the bow of the boat. When the wind steadied for a moment he reached up and began to untie the blanket sail.

Daniel continued to row, trying to keep the small boat steady as the sailor worked to untangle the lines. Although he had only a little experience with boats, Daniel worried that the wind was too strong for sailing. Still, he was afraid they would not make across if they could not beat the coming storm. Soon the sail sheet blew free, flapping wildly in the wind. A long arm of wood across the bottom of the sail bounced and swung in the waves, threatening to knock the sailor from the boat. Keeping his hand on the mast, the sailor slid down to the floor and grabbed a rope attached to the arm of the sail.

As soon as the sailor pulled on the line, the sail filled with wind and the boat shot forward. Daniel quickly pulled in his oars. They were sailing.

"Use an oar to help steer," the sailor yelled to Daniel. Holding an oar straight down in the water, Daniel tried to direct the boat which now raced north with the wind.

Just as they seemed under control, the wind changed directions. The sailor yelled for all to hold on as the long arm swung and the boat seemed to come to a sudden stop, momentarily left to flounder in the rough water. Even more suddenly than it stopped, the wind filled the sail again. They were now nearly flying over the water. Daniel strained to keep control of the oar he was using to steer. The small vessel leaned to one side, raising the other side out of the water. The wind dropped and then shifted again, pulling the arm and sail over the children's heads again. This time when the wind caught the sail the vessel leaned the other way. Daniel slid, putting his weight on the high side with the sailor, in an attempt to keep the boat from tipping.

Thunder that had rumbled from a distance began crashing overhead, accompanied by flashes of lightning. Above the howling wind they heard a loud slicing sound. A wall of rain was coming across the water toward them.

The children clung to one another, frozen with fear. Daniel could see the sailor was trying to outrun nature herself. Just a little farther, he thought. We are getting close to Canada.

The force of the wind grew as the wall of rain approached. Waves splashed in on them. The boat rode up on to the crest of each wave and came slamming down into the trough behind it.

"Hold on!" shouted Daniel. The children held tight to the seats. Suddenly they were pitched toward the bow as the boat ran aground in shallow water.

"We made . . .," the sailor's yell was drowned out by a bolt of lightning striking over their heads. The smell of burning wood filled the air as the mast split and shattered, toppling down, sail and all—

*   *   *   *   *

Mr. Daniels reached out his hand to the children. He was soaking wet.

"Malaika? Sammy? Are you all right?

"Malaika? Sammy? Take my hand. Let me help you. Are you O.K.?" Sammy sat up and pushed away the tree branch that had tumbled to the ground from the great oak above them. The rain continued to fall as if poured from the sky.

"Come on, children. Can you stand?"

Malaika blinked her eyes in confusion. What happened? Where was she? Where was Daniel?

"Malaika, it's Mr. Daniels. Can you stand? You were both knocked down when lightning hit the tree. A branch came down on you."

Sammy stood and shook the wet leaves off from him. He reached down and tried to pull his heavy backpack from the tangled mess. He was numb and cold and wanted to go home.

"Here, let me help you." Mr. Daniels grabbed a strap on the bag and pulled it free. Sammy's stuffed cat was still hanging from the pack.

"That was close. You two could have been really

hurt. When I came out of the school, I saw the busses were gone. I knew you must have missed your bus. When I turned the corner the wind and rain came up fast. I saw you running up under the tree and then the lightning hit it.

"Malaika, are you all right?"

Malaika nodded. She thought she was all right. She just couldn't think straight. Where was she? Daniel! Mr. Daniels? She wanted to go home.

"Come on, children. Come get in the car and out of the rain. I'll take you home to your mama. I'll bet she is worried sick about you two."

Going home to her mama was the best idea Malaika had heard in a long time. The two children and Mr. Daniels ran towards the car when Malaika remembered. "Wait! I have to go back!"

Sammy and Mr. Daniels went ahead and got in the car while Malaika ran back to the pile of tree limbs. She started searching through them. In the tangle of leaves and twigs was her ball of braided string. Picking it up and pushing it deep into her pocket she ran to the car. She was going home to Mama.

Glossary

a bad wind blows from the south.   Someone is in the area looking for runaway slaves.

abolitionist.   A person who demanded immediate emancipation or freeing of slaves.

bedlam.   A place of uproar.

bodice.   Top of a woman's dress or chemise.

baggage.   Code word for slaves escaping along the Underground Railroad.

britches.   Pants.

Brother Abraham.   Abraham Lincoln.

buckboard.   A horse-drawn vehicle comprised of flat boards on wheels.

buggy.   A small horse-drawn carriage.

cash bounty.   Money offered for the return of a runaway slave.

cat's cradle.   A game played by making various designs with a string threaded over one's fingers.

cobblestone.   Rounded stones used for paving.

coupled.   Linked together.

cyclone.   A severe storm with high winds.

da.   An Irish expression for father.

Dearborn.   A type of carriage.

Detroit River.   Last boundary crossed over by runaway slaves who were leaving the United States and traveling to Canada.

drinking gourd.   North Star.

emancipation car.   Underground railroad.

faithful groom.   Hitching post in the shape of a horse groom that was used as a guidepost to a safe house.

fire-eater.   A slave owner or someone supporting slavery.

forwarding.   Moving slaves from one safe location to another.

freedmen.   People who had once been slaves but were now free.

freedom line.   Underground railroad.

freedom road.   A runaway's route of travel.

freedom train.   Underground railroad.

Fugitive Slave Law. A law which allowed slaves who had escaped to free states to be captured and returned to their owners.

good book. The Bible.

gunger man. Someone who sells trinkets and small items like mirrors, pans, and watches.

grapevine. Method of communication where information is passed verbally from person to person.

haint. Ghost.

hardscrabble. Something which yields little but requires much hard work.

heaven. Canada.

line. Route of travel on the Underground Railroad.

load of potatoes. A wagon carrying runaway slaves.

lollygagging. Wasting time.

Mad River Rail. Railroad line in Indiana which operated during the 1850s.

mammy. A slave woman who cared for the master's children.

mercy mission. Helping fugitive slaves.

medallion.   An object resembling a medal.

Michigan Central.   Railroad line in Michigan which operated in the 1850s.

middle passage.   Route traveled between slavery and freedom.

Midnight.   Detroit, Michigan.

Negro.   An African-American person.

North Star.   The star Polaris which was often used by fugitive slaves as a guide toward the north.

Ohio River.   First river boundary crossed over by slaves into free states.

okra.   Vegetable with pods which are used in soups and stews.

overflow station.   Safe location that can hide several runaway slaves.

paddock.   A small fenced yard for horses.

parcels.   Runaway slaves.

placard.   Sign or notice which is posted in a public place.

pattyrollers.   People who patrolled roadways looking for runaway slaves.

pilot.   Guide for runaway slaves along the Underground Railroad.

prattie famine. A famine which occurred in Ireland and some other countries in the late 1840s when a disease ruined the potato crops and many people starved.

promised land. Canada.

Quaker. A religious group commonly called the Society of Friends.

red devils. Matches.

Republican Party. Started in 1854, it became one of two main political parties of the United States.

River Jordan. The Detroit River which was the final river crossed by slaves fleeing to Canada.

rods. A unit of measure equaling about 5-1\2 yards.

rollers. Cuts of trees used to skid boats onto shore.

safe haven. Safe place of hiding.

safe house. Safe place of hiding.

sanctuary. Safe place of hiding.

schooner. A large ship with two masts.

shepherd. Those that entice slaves to escape.

skull cap. A small brimless close-fitting cap.

slave haven. A safe place for runaway slaves to live.

Society of Friends. Organized membership of the Quakers.

special delivery. Delivery of an escaped slave to a station.

stationmaster. An owner of or person in charge of a safe hiding place.

submission. The condition of being controlled by someone else.

sulfur sticks. Matches.

surface line. Railroad route.

tatting. The process of making a kind of knotted lace.

to a friend from a friend. Something passed from one to another helper on the Underground Railroad.

trackless train. The Underground Railroad.

trap. Mouth.

Underground Railroad. A secret route of escape for runaway slaves from below the Mason-Dixon Line.

valet. A personal servant of the master.

venue.   A public auction.

vittles.   Food.

whitewash.   A liquid of quicklime and or chalk dust used for painting things white.

Underground Railroad Sites

Illinois
Elijah P. Lovejoy Monument and Gravesite, Alton, Illinois

Elijah Lovejoy was an abolitionist, minister, teacher, and the editor of the *Alton Observer*. Lovejoy called for immediate abolition. He was killed by a mob for his beliefs on November 7, 1837.

President Abraham Lincoln's Home (1844-1861) and National Historic Site, Springfield, Illinois

Lincoln had strong personal feelings against slavery. As President he invited Frederick Douglass, Sojourner Truth, and Martin R. Delaney to the White House.

Delaney was the first African-American to hold the rank of major during the Civil War. Delaney introduced a plan by which the routes of the Underground Railroad could be used to sneak Union soldiers behind Southern lines.

Michigan
George de Baptiste House, Detroit, Michigan
George de Baptiste created the Order of the African Mysteries with William Lambert. He devoted 32 years of his life to the Freedom Train.

Second Baptist Church, Detroit, Michigan
Organized in 1836, Second Baptist Church in Detroit is the oldest African-American Church in Michigan and is documented as a major station on the Underground Railroad. Reverend William Lambert was active in helping runaways for 32 years.

Sojourner Truth Gravesite, Oak Hill Cemetery, Battle Creek, Michigan
Sojourner became a leading abolitionist after her escape from slavery. She wandered the land telling of the plight of slaves and asking people to help destroy the institution of slavery. She died in 1883 at the age of 87, having lived to see the glory of emancipation.

Eratus Hussey's House-Sculpture, Battle Creek, Michigan

The sculpture is dedicated to the Underground Railroad, the African-American family, and Quaker Erstus Hussey and his wife Sarah. The sculpture is on the site of the Hussey's home which was a station in the Underground Railroad. The Hussey's served as stationmasters on the Underground Railroad for 20 years.

Ohio

The Rankin House, Ripley, Ohio

Reverend John Rankin, an educator and abolitionist, lived in this house which overlooks the Ohio River. It was the the first stop along the Underground Railroad for many slaves escaping from Kentucky. Runaways knew they had found the right house by a light left burning in an upstairs window.

In 1845 Rankin founded the Free Presbyterian Church of America which excluded slaveholders from membership and actively opposed slavery. He also establised an academy for African-American students.

Freedom Trail Stop, Xenia, Ohio
The people of this town opened their hearts and homes to those escaping along the Underground Railroad. There are a number of private homes in Xenia today that are well-known for their Underground Railroad activity over 100 years ago.

Wisconsin
The Milton House Museum, Milton, Wisconsin
In 1844 Joseph Goodrich built an unusual hexagon-shaped inn of poured concrete and hand-dug a tunnel from it. Travelers rested and ate in the tunnels before they journeyed across the state to Milwaukee or north to Canada. The Milton House is a state treasure with a brave and honorable history.

Indiana
Eliza Harris Marker, Pennville, Indiana
The marker and plaque commemorate the escape of Eliza Harris (Eliza from *Uncle Tom's Cabin*). Eliza planned her escape here across the Ohio River in her flight to freedom. Jumping from one ice floe to another across the icy river, she eventually escaped via the Underground Railroad.

Canada

North American Black Historical Museum and Cultural Center, Amherstburg, Ontario, Canada. This area was a settlement for runaways in the 1820s. Today the museum honors the Underground Railroad and focuses its exhibits on the influence the Underground Railroad had on Canadian history.

Sandwich First Baptist Church, Sandwich, Ontario, Canada
Escaped slaves made bricks from the clay of the Detroit River and built this church in 1844. It was an important part of the Underground Railroad. Many escaped slaves settled in the area.